LISTEN to THIS

JENNIFER BLECHER

LISTEN *to* THIS

GREENWILLOW BOOKS, an Imprint of HarperCollins Publishers

Listen to This

The text of this book is set in Iowan Old Style.
Book design by Sylvie Le Floc'h

Library of Congress Cataloging-in-Publication Data

Names: Blecher, Jennifer, author.
Title: Listen to this / by Jennifer Blecher.
Description: First edition. | New York : Greenwillow Books, an Imprint of HarperCollins Publishers, 2024. | Audience: Ages 8-12. | Audience: Grades 4-6. | Summary: Told from two perspectives, Lily and Will deal with the tumult of seventh grade including secrets, rumors, shifting friendships, overbearing parents, and a first dance.
Identifiers: LCCN 2023028132 (print) | LCCN 2023028133 (ebook) | ISBN 9780063140738 (hardcover) | ISBN 9780063140752 (ebook)
Subjects: CYAC: Middle schools—Fiction. | Schools—Fiction. | Friendship—Fiction. | Interpersonal relations—Fiction. | Family life—Fiction,
Classification: LCC PZ7.B61658 Li 2024 (print) | LCC PZ7.B61658 (ebook) | DDC [Fic]—dc23
LC record available at https://lccn.loc.gov/2023028132
LC ebook record available at https://lccn.loc.gov/2023028133
24 25 26 27 28 LBC 5 4 3 2 1
First Edition

 Greenwillow Books

To Steve and Amy Blecher

LISTEN *to* THIS

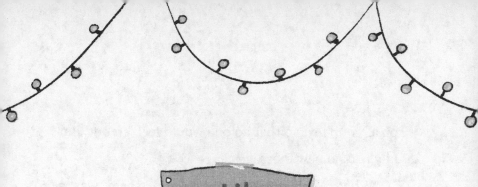

1. Lily

Lily and Maddie were sharing a bag of chips when Maddie's phone pinged with a new text. They weren't supposed to be on their phones during the school day. But at lunch, particularly when the weather was good and they could eat outside at their favorite grassy spot off the back courtyard, it was easy to sneak. Maddie pulled her phone from her backpack with one hand and reached for a chip with the other.

"What is it?" asked Lily.

Instead of tilting the phone so Lily could read along, Maddie smiled and scanned the screen. "One sec."

"Is it Sasha?"

Lily checked her own phone. Sasha was their other best friend. She had science in the tech wing before lunch and was often late. They always communicated on a group text so that no one would feel left out. But Lily had no new messages.

When Maddie finally looked up, there was a glimmer of excitement in her eyes. "It's not Sasha," she said. "But it is someone."

"*Someone?*" asked Lily.

Maddie nodded.

"Who? Tell me. Did you get asked to the dance? Is it Peter?" The first middle school dance of the year was in two weeks. In the past few days, the general rumbling of who might be going with a date had begun to get louder.

"What? No. Ew, Peter." Maddie shuddered.

Lily agreed. She'd once caught Peter digging his fingers under his socks and then smelling them. But he was kind of cute. And it's not like they were in Sienna's super-popular group and could go to the dance with gorgeous Theo or one of his friends. Lily, Maddie, and Sasha were in the middle, which was mostly good but sometimes felt like floating down a river in whatever direction the current ran. They planned to go to the dance as a group. But would the plan hold if one of them got asked by a boy?

Lily raised her eyebrows at Maddie. A silent plea. *Tell me.*

Maddie blushed. "It's just . . ."

The seconds piled up as Lily waited for Maddie to finish the sentence. Their spot in the shade of a large tree was so private, so quiet, that Lily could almost hear her heart pounding as she wondered if maybe it *was* Theo who'd texted Maddie to ask her to the dance. Sometimes Theo and Maddie warmed up together on the soccer field. They'd joke around as the ball sailed back and forth, both of them showing off their graceful fake-outs before charging toward the unattended goal while the other raced behind. Maddie knew that Lily had a crush on Theo. But it was a hopeless crush. The kind that would never amount to anything. They barely even spoke.

Still, would Maddie actually say yes to Theo?

"It's not a text from a boy," said Maddie. "It's from a girl."

"Okay," said Lily, both relieved that the text wasn't

from Theo and confused as to why Maddie was acting so strange.

"A girl from camp," continued Maddie. "Bex. Her real name is Rebecca, but we all call her Bex. She's not a long-name person. She's a short-name person. So yeah, Bex." Maddie always rambled when she was nervous, like before a vocab quiz when she stood in the hallway desperately trying to make sentences from the color-coded flash cards that Lily let her borrow.

"Bex," repeated Lily. "Is she the one with the calligraphy pen?"

"Yes! That's her. You remembered."

"She started all your letters. They were perfect. I saved them."

Lily loved handwriting, pens, and delicate-tipped markers. She had long ago perfected her own signature, always ending her name with a tiny ink flower above the outer tip of the y, and she was helping Maddie and Sasha come up with cool ideas for their own names. It was not going well. Maddie lacked the patience to get her lettering consistent, and Sasha always goofed halfway through, crossing out her attempt only to make another mistake on the next try. But every letter that Maddie had sent from sleepover camp began with Lily's name in big looping letters that were both thick and crisp, which was a tricky combination.

When she'd arrived home, Maddie had explained that a girl in her cabin had written the "Dear Lily" part. Lily had been flattered that someone had taken so much care with her name. Now, however, she wondered if this girl, Bex, had written "Dear Lily" and handed the letter back to Maddie to finish, or if she'd stayed next to Maddie, looking over her shoulder as Maddie wrote about dripping wax on her T-shirts before dipping them in dye, and the new music her favorite counselor played in the afternoons. Something in Maddie's expression made Lily think that Bex had read every word.

"I like her," said Maddie.

"Okay," said Lily. Maddie was allowed to have other friends. But did her other friend have to be so talented at the one thing that Lily was good at? Did she have to text Maddie at lunch, which was their only time to really talk during the school day? Lily wished she was cooler than to have these dumb, jealous thoughts. But ever since Maddie and Sasha had made the regional elite soccer team, Lily had begun to worry about all the time they would be spending without her. All their inside jokes, matching gear, and new soccer teammates would tilt the even balance of their friendship. There was no way around it.

"No," continued Maddie. "I mean, I like Bex in a different way."

"Like, *like* her?"

Maddie nodded. She bit her lower lip. "I think so."

Lily didn't know how to respond. If the text had been from Peter, or maybe even Theo, she would have immediately grabbed Maddie's phone and started scrolling back through every single exchange. Maddie would have sat beside her, their shoulders pressed tight, while they overanalyzed each word and emoji, then worked together to come up with the perfect reply. They might have even forgotten to finish eating. But this particular secret slowed Lily's response instead of speeding it up.

"Are you going out with her?" asked Lily. "With Bex?" It was a question at the top of a mountain of other questions. Like: Are you gay? What does it feel like? How do you know? Have you kissed her? Does it change anything for us?

"We're just friends for now," said Maddie. "But we both know that we like each other. We talked about it this summer right before camp ended."

Maddie had returned from sleepover camp three months ago. That was almost twelve weeks of seventh grade. Twelve weekends of sleepovers with Sasha where they watched makeup tutorials on YouTube and recorded viral dance routines in dorky striped knee socks. It was hundreds of texts and countless hours of strategic planning about the dance. Throughout it all, Maddie had never mentioned having feelings for Bex.

"Don't tell anyone," said Maddie. "I'm not embarrassed or anything. It's just tricky to say out loud. Like, it's hard to know when to tell people."

"Do your parents know?"

Maddie shook her head. "Not yet."

"Does Sasha?"

"You're the only one. Well, besides Bex." Maddie smiled as she texted a quick response and then slid the phone into her backpack. "Can I have another chip?"

Lily had forgotten all about the chips in her hand. She tilted the bag toward Maddie, wishing she knew the next right thing to say.

Just then, a hand pressed down on Lily's shoulder. "Boo," said Sasha as she jumped in between them.

"It's not scary when it's always you," said Maddie.

"Whatever," said Sasha. "You guys are just so lucky that you're *not* me. I had the worst morning. Like, it's only lunch and I'm already done with the entire day. Seriously, I deserve to go home. Someone call me a limo."

Lily and Maddie locked eyes and laughed. Lily had never been more grateful for Sasha's dramatic form of distraction.

"Let me guess," said Lily as Sasha pulled out her food. "Jake?"

Sasha used to have a huge crush on Jake. But over the summer he'd morphed into a jerk who stole ice pops from the pool snack bar and flipped off the lifeguards when they called him out for doing somersaults off the diving board. Now Sasha couldn't stand him, which was unfortunate because they had most of their classes together.

"Yes, Jake!" answered Sasha. "We had to be lab partners. And just like always, he tried on both pairs of safety goggles and then picked the one he liked best, handing me the reject that had his gross nose oil on it."

As Sasha kept talking, describing how Jake flicked something into the air that looked suspiciously like it came from inside his body, Lily's attention drifted. When would Maddie tell Sasha about Bex? When Sasha finished ranting about Jake? Or maybe later, like at dismissal? They were past the age of pinkie swears and solemn promises to share every single thing, but this was big. Sasha had to know.

Lily unscrewed the cap of her teal water bottle and took a sip. When Maddie's face grew serious, Lily assumed she was about to tell. Instead, Maddie nodded toward the courtyard where most of their grade sat and whispered, "Beep, beep, beep. Drama detector alert."

Lily looked over her shoulder to see Sienna, the leader of the popular group, walking toward them with a spiral notebook tucked under her arm and a pen in her hand. Sometimes, when Lily looked in the mirror after brushing her teeth at night, she gathered her hair in one hand and tilted her chin from side to side, imagining how it would feel to see Sienna's reflection instead of her own. Sienna's sparkling eyes. Her clear skin. Her glossy lips that were always bubbling with important information about who'd just said something embarrassing, hilarious, amazing, or pathetic. Sienna could distinguish between the options in an instant, while Lily was often left debating which was which.

"Question," said Sienna as soon as she reached their lunch spot. "Who do you each want to go with to the dance? I'm keeping track to make everything easier. You know, for everyone."

"Wow, Sienna," said Maddie sarcastically. "That's so nice of you."

"Really sweet," added Sasha.

Sienna sighed. "Whatever, guys. Don't blame me when things get really messed up."

"We won't," said Maddie.

"FYI, Maddie," said Sienna, returning Maddie's smirk. "I was going to put you with Theo. I know for a fact that he likes you. But I'm sure I can find someone else for him to go with. It'll be super easy."

Lily did not move, not one single centimeter. But on the inside, everything lurched. It was official: Theo liked Maddie. What new revelation was going to crash into her life next? Would Maddie reveal that Bex lived a few towns away and invite her to the dance? Would Sasha reverse her stance on Jake and suddenly like him again? Would Lily be the only one without a date? What would she do then?

As Sienna walked away, Maddie and Sasha looked at each other and nodded. Lily exhaled in relief. Of course their threesome would stick together. No matter what know-it-all Sienna claimed, nothing was going to change their plan of going to the dance as a group.

Except then Maddie said, "Lily, we have to tell you something."

"Don't be mad at us," added Sasha.

"What is it?" asked Lily, suddenly confused. "Tell me."

"We can't go to the dance," said Maddie. "You know how we have that big Jubilee tournament for elites? They had to move it up a weekend because Penn State made the NCAA finals so they need the field to host Delaware. Jubilee got pushed and now it's the same weekend as the dance. Our coach thinks we'll easily make the last round on Sunday, so . . ."

Who made what?

Lily had tuned out somewhere around "Delaware," but she got the point. Maddie and Sasha were going to be away the weekend of the dance! Lily hadn't deserved to make the elite team. She hadn't scored a single goal the whole regular soccer season, and she stunk at defense. When Coach Brennan yelled her name to sub her out of games, she didn't get annoyed like Maddie or miss the call because she was so focused on the next play like Sasha. Instead, Lily sprinted to the sidelines, relieved to be part of the cheering squad, not the one under pressure to perform. But now she wished that she'd gotten to practice early to work on ball control, or held her planks all the way until the whistle blew. Maybe then Coach Brennan would have recommended her for elites and she wouldn't be facing the prospect of attending the dance all alone.

There were other girls she could go to the dance with, of course. Maybe Nora or Allie. But it wouldn't be the same. Plans could change in an instant. Nora might decide to meet other kids for pizza before the dance and forget to tell Lily. Or Allie might suddenly agree to go with Kyle, who was obsessed with her, and leave Lily hanging. The number of ways it could go wrong were infinite.

"I'm not going without you guys," decided Lily. "I'll skip the dance. It's fine."

"You can't skip the dance," said Maddie. "You've been talking about it for weeks."

Cheek-burning embarrassment rarely happened with Maddie and Sasha. Not even when Lily tripped over sidewalk curbs, or Maddie snorted chocolate milkshake through her nose, or Sasha mixed up her words, calling her brother "shellfish" instead of "selfish." Those things caused laughter and inside jokes about seafood that didn't make sense to anyone else in the world. But now Lily was genuinely humiliated by how much time she'd spent talking about the dance. Didn't she have anything better to think about?

The bell rang, announcing five minutes until the end of lunch. Sasha looked from the school building to Lily and back. "Ugh," she said. "Double, triple, quadruple ugh. I have math, otherwise I'd totally stay." Sasha was one of the few seventh graders who'd placed into advanced eighth-grade math. She liked to get to class early to claim a seat in the front.

"Go be a math genius," said Maddie. "I'll stay with Lily."

"No," said Lily, standing. "Let's all go."

She didn't want to sit there a second longer, embarrassment pooling all around her. As she gathered her stuff, Lily scrunched the empty bag of chips in her fist, wishing that she could also crush the growing ache inside her chest.

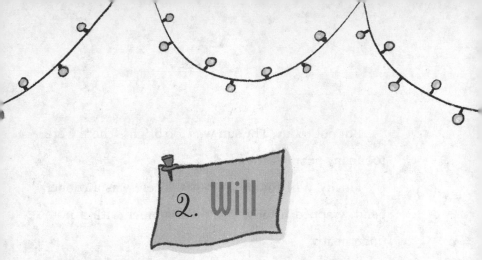

2. Will

Will reached into the front pocket of his backpack, searching for his Power Putty, while he waited for Gavin to meet him at lunch. There were over thirty muscles in the hand. Squeezing putty was a good way to work them.

Even though Will was sitting outside a school building of flat surfaces and ninety-degree angles, part of his mind was always on rock climbing.

Handholds. Foot crevices. Strength. Balance.

He was probably the only student who could leap for the overhang above the school's back entrance and scale the entire three stories using only the window frames and gutters for support.

Someday he was going to give it a try. And it would be epic.

But not today. The sun was too bright. There were too many people around.

Finally Will found the putty. There was a rubber band wrapped around the tin container with a note underneath.

Strange. Had someone slipped the note there during one of his morning classes? Was it possibly from a girl?

The chances of that were slim. But the upcoming dance was making everything weird. The dance was like chalk dust floating in a climbing gym—always there, even when not explicitly noticed.

Will unfolded the note. He immediately recognized the handwriting.

It was from his dad.

Good luck on your math quiz today! Don't forget to double-check your work!

Will rolled his eyes and shoved the note to the bottom of his bag.

Honestly, his dad should be thanking him for

messing up in math. Paying him, even.

If Will was a perfect child with a wheelie backpack filled with advanced textbooks and Science Olympiad permission slips, what would his dad talk about on his podcast? What would the hundreds of thousands of *Dr. Dad* listeners possibly learn about raising kids? What stories would they laugh at as they drove to work because Will's dad talking about what it was like to be a single father was so freaking hilarious?

Will scooped the putty from the container.

He squeezed. Hard.

It was ten minutes into lunch. Theo, Jake, and their soccer-obsessed crew were kicking a ball around the courtyard. Sienna and her minions sat at a picnic table, hunched over a spiral notebook. Lily, Maddie, and Sasha were in a tight-knit girl huddle under the tree. The gamers, the mathletes, the artists, the musicians. Everyone was with their people.

Where was Gavin?

If Will unpacked his lunch before Gavin got there, he'd look like a loser eating all alone. But there was also a chance Gavin would never show. It wouldn't be the first time a teacher had made Gavin stay late for a special talk. In which case, Will would be a very hungry loser.

Being in seventh grade was like climbing a smooth rock face with no safety ropes.

Every action mattered. Every choice meant something.

Be too independent, and you're a loner.

Be too funny, and you're annoying.

Be too obvious, and you're obnoxious.

Be too oblivious, and you're plain old stupid.

Which was what Will's dad and his bazillion podcast listeners would never understand. Acting like he didn't care required an enormous amount of caring.

Will was about to unwrap his sandwich when someone shoved him from behind. A what's-up push. Not a get-out-of-the-way push.

Gavin, finally. Will's best friend who Will didn't like very much. Will appreciated that Gavin was somebody to sit next to at lunch and watch climbing videos with after school. But as soon as Gavin opened his mouth to speak, Will had the urge to scoot away from him.

Only then who would Will sit with?

"Prince William," said Gavin as he bumped his shoulder into Will's and held out his phone. "Are you prepared to have your mind blown? I'm talking brain bits splattered all the way to the clouds. This is it, man."

Gavin's new thing was pulling audio clips from the *Dr. Dad* podcast and splicing them with videos of old ladies from ancient TV shows. It was probably illegal, the kind of thing that his dad's podcast producer would be able to shut down in a heartbeat with legal words like *copyright* and *digital piracy*.

But Gavin never got more than thirty views on his videos. So Will had decided it wasn't worth being the kind of kid who told on his best friend.

Gavin pressed Play. A video began of an old lady with tightly curled white hair answering a pink telephone that was mounted to the wall.

"So I open the school calendar," played his dad's

voice, which was synced to the woman's mouth. "And I see the words *middle school dance* printed right there, clear as day. I turn to Will and I ask, 'Son, are you planning to go to the dance?' And he looks at me like I've got a third eye. And I'm thinking to myself, *If this boy doesn't go to this darn school dance . . .*"

His dad's voice cut out right as the old woman on the screen took the phone from her ear and began banging it against the wall, screaming, "I'm going to kill him. I'm going to kill him. I'm going to kill him."

"Funny, right?" asked Gavin as he exited the video.

"Hilarious."

"Knew you'd like it. I just put it together last night. I hope this is the one."

Will smiled and raised his chin. It was a silent agreement because agreeing in actual words was impossible. Gavin's biggest goal—for one of his videos to go viral—was Will's worst nightmare.

A ton of kids at school knew about *Dr. Dad*. But as far as Will could tell, none of them had taken the time to actually listen to a full episode. They mostly hassled Will about being famous and whether he wore his hair long and shaggy to dodge the paparazzi, which confirmed Will's suspicion that they were clueless about the podcast's subject matter.

Even Gavin hadn't listened until last year, when he and his mom were stuck in traffic on the highway. They'd had plenty of time to listen to the entire episode about how long it took Will to stop wetting the bed.

From that point on, Gavin had become a loyal listener.

"And dude," continued Gavin as he cued up a new file. "Look at this video I made with the intro."

"What intro?"

"To your dad's podcast. You know, the whole 'You are my sunshine, my only sunshine' thing. It's audio gold."

That whole *thing* was a recording of Will's mom singing to him before bed. She'd made it just a few weeks before she died, when Will was in third grade. Will had the entire recording saved on his phone. Sometimes he played it at night and, if he concentrated hard enough, he could almost feel his mom's finger brushing his arm and her lips resting against the top of his head.

Now, of course, the song was also something else entirely. Part of a lead-in to the story of her death that introduced every *Dr. Dad* episode.

Will was almost used to hearing it.

But not in the middle of school lunch.

Not alongside Gavin's jazz hands and his psyched smile. Or the high pitch of his mocking voice.

Something deep inside Will snapped.

He grabbed Gavin's phone and chucked it across the courtyard like a Frisbee.

As the phone sailed along, Will prayed that it would shatter into a million pieces. He wanted whatever electronic panel that allowed his mom's voice to exist in Gavin's palm to crack on impact. Never to play again.

Instead, the phone skidded to a pathetic stop on the grass and landed right at the feet of Mr. Stanlow, one of the middle school guidance counselors and Will's homeroom advisor.

Mr. Stanlow crouched down in his jeans and high-top sneakers. He picked up the phone, looked right at Will, and said, "What a lovely surprise. And it's not even my birthday."

"Crap," said Gavin. "You're in for it."

Will said nothing. He just followed Mr. Stanlow into the school building and straight to his first-floor office.

"You go first," said Mr. Stanlow once they'd both settled into their seats. Mr. Stanlow was behind his desk, and Will was in an old leather armchair that was decorated with scratch marks from all the kids who'd sat there before him.

"Sorry?" said Will.

"And . . . ?"

"And it won't happen again?"

"Because . . . ?"

"Because it won't?" said Will.

Mr. Stanlow sighed as he twisted off the lid of a glass canister that was filled with individually wrapped lollipops and slid it across his desk. "You're better than this, Will. You're in my homeroom, for crying out loud. You're a Stanlowian! We've got a reputation to uphold around here."

Will smiled. Mr. Stanlow was definitely the coolest of the homeroom advisors and, cheesy as it was, Will was proud to be in his group. After someone mysteriously left a Pinkie Pie figurine on Mr. Stanlow's desk one morning, everyone in their advisory adopted My Little Pony code names. Will's was Rainbow Dash. He answered to it every morning when Mr. Stanlow took attendance.

"Thanks," muttered Will as he pulled a lollipop from the canister. Blue raspberry. His favorite.

"Care to tell me what inspired you to throw Gavin's cell phone across the courtyard?"

"Not really."

"I'm here to listen, Will. And help. It's literally my job."

Will dropped his gaze and focused on folding the lollipop wrapper in his lap.

"All right then," said Mr. Stanlow as he swiveled his chair to face his computer and began typing. "Clearly I've got no choice but to check in with my pony chat groups while you gather your thoughts."

"I heard Apple Bloom might be working for the dark side," said Will. "Just a tip."

For a second the joke worked. Mr. Stanlow stopped typing what was obviously a note in Will's school file and began laughing. But instead of riffing on the joke like he normally might, Mr. Stanlow leaned back in his chair, locked his eyes on Will, and said absolutely nothing.

If Will could have put the sludge that was filling his chest—that was on the verge of oozing up his throat—into words, he would have considered saying those words to Mr. Stanlow. The guy was youngish, and cool. In addition to a collection of My Little Pony figurines, he had a half-empty bottle of sriracha on his bookshelf.

But Will couldn't find a way to describe the deep humiliation that came from his dad sharing the private details of his life for laughs. Or the betrayal he felt when his mom's lullaby played for anyone in the world to hear.

Sometimes, all the embarrassment and the disloyalty did him in.

So yeah, he snapped. He did something stupid.

That didn't mean he owed Mr. Stanlow an emotional confession.

"So can I go now?" asked Will when it became obvious that Mr. Stanlow was not going to break his stare. "What's my punishment? Recycling?"

At the beginning of the year, when he and Gavin got in trouble for pouring water over each other's heads in the school hallway, Mr. Stanlow made them empty the classroom recycling bins for a week.

Instead of answering, however, Mr. Stanlow stood and unlocked an upper cabinet door. "Actually, I've got a different idea. And I think you're going to enjoy it."

Mr. Stanlow took down a white Polaroid camera and handed it to Will.

"What is this?" asked Will. "A present? Is it graduation already?"

Mr. Stanlow smiled. "Sort of. You've graduated from my normal bag of tricks to the big leagues. Congratulations."

As Will examined the camera, Mr. Stanlow explained the new "How I See It" campaign, where a few students each week would shoot one pack of Polaroid film to document how they saw life at school. The pictures would then be displayed on the bulletin board outside the guidance office.

"You'll be one of the first," said Mr. Stanlow. "Which makes you a trendsetter."

Will shook his head and placed the camera on Mr. Stanlow's desk. "No thanks. I'll take recycling."

"No can do, Will. I want you to open your eyes. Look at what's going on out there in the wonderful world of middle school. Who knows? Maybe something will spark your interest."

Will huffed sarcastically.

Mr. Stanlow ignored him. "You've got two weeks to complete the assignment," he continued. "And you need to show me some real effort with this one or I'm going to have to call your dad."

Great. Will's dad would definitely spin any call from school into a podcast episode. Maybe Mr. Stanlow could be his guest. They could compare notes on trying to get Will to open up. To expand his horizons. To see the world in a bright, new, sparkly light.

Anything was better than that.

A bell rang, signaling the end of lunch. Will grabbed the camera. What choice did he have? He would zip it into his backpack and forget about it for a while. Except Will realized that he'd left his backpack outside.

"Go fast," said Mr. Stanlow. "If you're late to class, I'll take the blame."

By the time Will reached the courtyard, the place was deserted except for his backpack and a bright teal water bottle.

Lily's water bottle. It had a white sticker that read STRONG IS THE NEW PRETTY in bold black letters. She had a habit of putting the water bottle on her desk and tracing the letters with her index finger when things got slow in Spanish.

She must have left it by accident. Spanish was their next class, so Will grabbed the bottle and headed back toward the school building.

It was only when Will approached the classroom door, late and out of breath, that he realized his mistake. Lily's seat was right in front of Sienna's.

He couldn't just walk up to Lily and hand her the water bottle. Sienna's hawk eyes would never miss something like that. Before the end of the day, half the grade would think that Will had a crush on Lily and he'd stolen her water bottle just to have an excuse to talk to her.

Or maybe ask her to the dance.

Will put the water bottle in his backpack and then slid into his seat.

He had no plans to go to the dance. And he definitely did not intend to be the star of the Sienna gossip show.

Lily would survive without her water bottle. She had friends to walk her to the dispenser.

Will pulled out his Power Putty and kneaded it beneath the cover of his desk. The tacky substance was meant to strengthen his grip. But sometimes, it was just as useful at helping him survive.

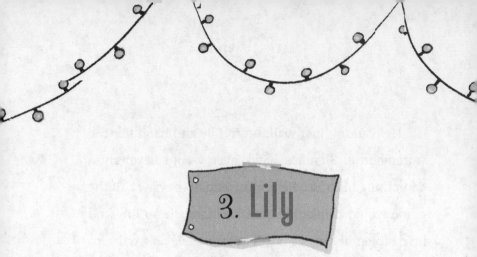

3. Lily

At the end of the school day, Lily met up with Maddie and Sasha in the grass by the side parking lot. Maddie and Sasha were waiting for Sasha's mom to drive them to soccer practice and, after they left, Lily was going to walk home. As Lily sat down beside Maddie's black soccer bag, she wondered if Maddie was going to tell Sasha about Bex. Or maybe she already had? Was that why they were both so unusually quiet?

But then Sasha checked the time on her phone and fell onto her back in frustration, and Lily realized that they were just nervous about being late. Their coach for the elite team was super strict, not like Coach Brennan with her whistle malfunctions and focus on "teamwork making the dream work." As Sasha rechecked the time on her phone and Maddie leaned over to get a better view down the street, they began discussing Riley's knee injury and whether Kareena would step up and play goalie even though she preferred defense.

It was like Lily wasn't even there. Until Maddie looked over at her and asked, "What's up with the grass murder?"

Lily froze, a single blade of grass torn halfway down the middle in her fingers. Next to her right knee was a bare patch of ground. Next to her left knee, a pile of shredded green. Lily hadn't meant to pull out that much grass. It was just so satisfying to split the blades in two while she waited for the soccer talk to end.

"Grass can be evil," said Sasha. "Ever heard of grass stains? What if Lily's just trying to save the white pants of the world?"

"Good point," said Maddie. "How did I not think of that?"

Lily smiled. Maybe now they would actually include her in their conversation. Except Sasha's mom rounded the corner. Maddie and Sasha jumped up.

"Sorry, girls," said Sasha's mom as she rolled

down the car window. "Oven issues."

Sasha mouthed this last part in perfect unison with her mom. "Oven issues" meant her mom had simply lost track of time. In addition to working at a local bakery, she'd recently started her own business making custom cupcake sculptures. Sasha said it was to cover the elite team expenses, so she tried not complain when her mom was late. As Maddie and Sasha threw their backpacks and soccer gear into the trunk, Sasha's mom smiled at Lily.

"Hey, Lils. How you doing, honey?"

Lily shrugged. It was all she could manage as the rear car doors slammed shut.

"Come here, sweetheart," said Sasha's mom. She opened a large plastic container that was resting on the front passenger seat and handed Lily a vanilla cupcake with strawberry frosting. With her other hand, she squeezed Lily's wrist. "Love ya, kid."

Lily forced a tight smile. It was only after they drove away, Maddie and Sasha waving wildly from the back seat, that Lily realized who the rest of the cupcakes in the container were for—the elite team. Riley and

Kareena and all the other girls she didn't know.

With a giant stretch of empty afternoon in front of her, Lily began to walk home. She peeled the wrapper from the cupcake, took one huge bite, and then threw the rest in a sidewalk trash can. It wasn't nearly as satisfying as she'd hoped. By the time she was halfway home, regretting having thrown the cupcake away more and more with each passing block, Lily decided she needed a sugar boost.

On Lily's side of the street was City Convenience, where she liked to buy bags of sour watermelon gummies. On the other side was the Secret Coffee Shop. Lily couldn't remember exactly when kids in her grade switched from bumping into each other in the candy aisle to standing next to each other in line for drinks with complicated names. But it had definitely happened. It wasn't embarrassing to be caught buying candy; it was just cooler to be spotted getting coffee. Lily crossed the street.

Inside the front door of the Secret Coffee Shop was an enormous bulletin board that ran from the floor to the ceiling. Next to the board, in a basket, were blank index cards and colored gel pens. Customers were supposed to write down their secrets and post them to the board. In just that day alone, Lily had collected several new secrets. Other people's, like Maddie having romantic feelings for a girl named Bex, and her own, like how devastated she was to learn that Maddie and Sasha would be missing the dance. Sometimes—okay *most* times— her day was just as likely to be filled with secrets as with truths.

Lily scanned the cards. They were written in all different colors and handwriting styles. There were funny ones, like:

I must confess, it was I who stole the last cookie from the box.

Is it wrong to love my dog more than my boyfriend?

Everyone poops. But to the unlucky person who was behind me in the bathroom line, my sincere apologies.

And some were super sad, like:

My wife died four years ago and I still talk to her every morning and every evening.

This is the only place in the whole city where people say hello to me.

Some days it's hard to keep on going on. Today is one of those days.

Every once in a while, Lily was tempted to write down a secret and stick it on the board. But whenever she got close, imagining what color gel pen would match the particular secret—like red for one best friend having a new secret crush, or neon green for how much it hurt to watch her two best friends drive away without her— fear stopped her. What if someone from school saw? Or recognized her handwriting? What if her secrets were stupid? Not worthy of a bulletin board in a cool coffee shop where people with nose piercings typed on laptops?

Lily was about to step away from the board to order a drink when she heard "Hey, Lily."

It was Sienna. Beautiful, popular, all-knowing Sienna. Thank goodness Lily hadn't written down one of her secrets. Maddie's "beep, beep, beep, drama detector" warning echoed in her mind.

"Don't you just love this board?" continued Sienna. "I could stand here all day. Learning people's secrets is just, like, fun. It makes me happy. On the inside."

Lily tried to think of the right response. Fast. When it came to Sienna, there was always a right and a wrong. If Lily answered correctly, maybe Sienna would interrupt her to say, "Oh my gosh, Lily, it just occurred to me. Why don't *you* go to the dance with Theo. You two would be perfect together. I can't believe I didn't think of that before." Sienna would whip out her spiral notebook and write Lily's name next to Theo's. Maybe she would even slide the paper across the table so Lily could draw her signature flower at the end of the *y*.

Instead, all Lily managed was: "Me, too. Super happy."

Sienna smiled. "I knew you'd understand. Unlike my mom who is *such* a buzzkill. Whenever we come in here, she's all like, 'Sienna, do you get it now? Do you see how tough it is out there and why we always have to be kind to everyone, even strangers?' Like this board of other people's secrets is supposed to bum me out. Or scare me. Or teach me some uber-important life lesson. Because apparently seventh grade is so ridiculously easy. As if *she* has any idea what we deal with all day."

"My mom's the same way," lied Lily. Her mom was actually obsessed with her home coffee maker and rarely stepped inside the Secret Coffee Shop. But Lily wanted to keep the conversation going. Maybe there was a reason Sienna was getting an after-school drink all alone, without her normal crew of Cora and Audrey? Maybe they had more in common than Lily realized?

As she stepped forward in line, Lily pretended to study the chalkboard menu while Sienna scrolled on her phone. Then suddenly, Sienna nudged Lily, one finger hovering over her screen. "This is your big sister, right?"

Lily nodded. On Sienna's phone was ReesesPieces, the Instagram account where Lily's sister, Reese, posted photos of her fashion finds and gave advice for styling outfits.

"She has such cool style," said Sienna. "I just started following her. I love how she's trendy but not, like, drowning in trends." Sienna tapped on Reese's profile to see the full grid of old posts. Among the squares of Reese in different outfits was a photograph of Lily. "Wait. OMG. Is this *you*?"

Sienna tapped on the image of Lily wearing an oversized chunky cardigan sweater and cut-off jeans with wool socks bunched around her ankles. A stack of fashion coffee table books and her mom's tortoiseshell reading glasses were arranged at Lily's side. Reese had posted the image last year, right before high school finals. The caption read: "Hitting the books. Just not the right books."

"You look so cool," said Sienna, as her eyes moved from the image to Lily and back. "I'm getting coastal grandma vibes mixed with funky librarian. Nice."

Lily smiled, flattered at the way Sienna implied that she was somehow responsible for the result when it had been entirely Reese's vision and her choice of clothes. All Lily had done was follow instructions on how to tilt her chin and fold her legs. "Reese loves to style people," said Lily. "She wants to go into fashion."

"Same," said Sienna. "I love fashion. Hey, want to get our drinks and sit for a sec?"

"Sure," answered Lily. "Totally."

They chose two empty seats at the wooden counter that ran the length of the front window. Sienna let out her messy ponytail before unwrapping her paper straw and plunging it into her drink. As she leaned forward, the pendant on her necklace slipped from beneath the neckline of her shirt. It was an evil-eye necklace that Lily had admired but never seen this close. The center stone was real turquoise, with swirls of white and a bumpy texture. The black eyelashes were carved into a silver setting, and there were tiny diamonds at both corners of the eye. The necklace was delicate and pretty, but also grown-up and mysterious. Lily wanted to reach out and touch it.

"I love your necklace," said Lily.

"Oh, thanks." Sienna shrugged. "I got it online. I can send you the link. Maybe Reese will like it, too.

Just don't get the exact same one or anything."

"No, I know," promised Lily. "I'd never do that."

Sienna smiled. "I trust you."

Lily smiled back. She didn't say *thank you* out loud, but she did think it. Sienna trusted her. Maybe she even liked her. The afternoon, the next day, and all the days to follow brightened with possibility. What if they became friends? What if Sienna set her up with a date for the dance and they got ready together? What if Lily no longer spent her afternoons waiting for Maddie and Sasha to get picked up for soccer and instead missed their calls because she was hanging out with . . . Sienna?

"I have your number somewhere," said Sienna as she woke her phone. "But can you give it to me one more time?"

As Lily recited her number, watching to make sure that Sienna entered it correctly, Sienna ignored an incoming group text from Cora and Audrey. If Lily had to write one secret on an index card that very instant, she would choose a pink gel pen and write the words: *I really hope that Sienna texts.*

4. Will

It was Wednesday. A climbing day.

Will sat on a wooden bench in the locker room of the Philly Rocks climbing gym and kicked off his sneakers.

Across the room, Gavin stood on an identical bench. He balanced on one foot, pretending to fall as he windmilled his arms for dramatic effect.

"Dude," called Gavin. "Here. Shoot me like this."

Ever since Will had made the mistake of telling Gavin about the "How I See It" assignment, Gavin had been posing in all kinds of stupid situations—with his head in a trash can, his body wedged in a closing door, a knit hat pulled down over his face.

It didn't matter that Will had left the Polaroid camera at home that morning. Gavin was oblivious to those kind of important details.

Will rolled his eyes. He'd played along at school, agreeing that at least one of his shots had to take place in the boys' bathroom. But now the joke was getting old. "Give it up, Gavin," he said. "I'm not wasting film on you."

"Wasting?" said Gavin. "This shot would be a gift. Someday, when I'm on the cover of *Climbing*, they'll take your dinky little Polaroid picture and set it next to an epic shot of me free soloing El Capitan. Don't worry. I'll make sure they give you photo credit. You know, just so you can see how it feels to have your name in the magazine."

"Keep dreaming," said Will.

Gavin hopped down. "Don't need to. I'm wide-awake."

As Will slid on his climbing shoes, he wondered if maybe his whole life was a dream. How else could he explain the ever-present sensation of being one step out of sync with everyone around him?

With Gavin, Will was one step ahead. Either waiting for Gavin to get a clue and catch up, or increasing his speed in the hopes of leaving Gavin in the dust.

With his dad, Will was one step to the side. They lived right up against each other, but there was an invisible wall between them that refused to crumble.

With his classmates, Will was one step behind. Watching from the back of the crowd to see where the herds were going next, always surprised by the twists and turns they took.

Will wished he could find someone to walk with. Not in a holding hands, skipping off into the sunset kind of way. Just someone he could wave goodbye to and trust that they'd be back the next day, moving at the same pace.

But how was he supposed to find that person?

Will was surrounded by people. The events of his life were known by millions. His dad had a whole folder of printed emails and DMs that *Dr. Dad* fans had written to Will about their own experiences with loss, resilience, and childhood. His dad was certain that Will would want to read them when he was older and could finally appreciate those sorts of things.

Unlikely.

Will walked out of the locker room. Alone.

"Prince William," called Gavin. "Wait up! I'm on belay."

Will kept going. Down the hall and out to the spring climbing floor.

The angled gray walls were creviced like recently unfolded origami paper. Pink, purple, blue, and green grips decorated their length. Sometimes, right before a climb, Will was tempted to scream his name just to hear how his voice would sound as it bounced off the fifty-foot-tall ceilings.

But he would never do it. At Philly Rocks, Will was focused. He was, as his dad often said on his podcast, his best Will-self.

Will stretched, then chalked his hands. He stepped into his harness and secured his carabiners. He checked the board where instructors paired off climbers. Gavin was right; he was on belay for Will's climbs.

Gavin liked to psych Will out as he held the safety ropes. Daring him to leap for difficult holds that were beyond his reach. "Do it, do it, do it," Gavin would chant.

Whatever. At a certain point, Will's brain went quiet and he could zone Gavin out.

Will charted the wall. He pictured his body scaling from one hold to the next. There were a few paths that he could take to reach the top. The decision was his alone.

Three, two, one. Gavin hit the stopwatch. And Will began to climb.

He struggled a bit with the center sequence but made pretty good time. When he hit the buzzer at the top, Will knew he'd given it his all.

Dustin, the owner of Philly Rocks, was waiting at the bottom when Will rappelled down. "Nice climb," said Dustin. "Solid choices. But you can do better." He looked at Gavin. "How about I take over?"

Dustin spent a lot of time behind the desk, leaving the junior coaches to staff the climbing floor. So when Dustin took over on belay, focusing his attention on Will alone, Will didn't zone anything out. He climbed *and* listened.

Will did the same wall three times in a row, all under Dustin's guidance.

Each time the climb was smoother. Fewer holds and less hesitation.

When Will finally slid his feet from the tight grip of his shoes, his muscles were beat but his heart was light.

He couldn't wait to tell his dad how well he'd done.

Except when he walked out of Philly Rocks, his dad wasn't standing outside talking to Gavin's mom. Stephanie was.

"Hey," called Stephanie, waving at Will. "There's my favorite guy in the whole entire world."

Stephanie opened her arms. Even though Will had recently shifted from giving Stephanie a full-on front hug to more of a sideways around-the-shoulders kind of hug, he leaned into her.

Stephanie was a lot of things: his mom's college roommate, her forever best friend, the only person Will was allowed to get in a car with without prior permission from his dad.

Oh yeah, and she was also Sienna's mother.

Will peered into the backseat of Stephanie's car.

Yep. There was Sienna, typing into her phone.

"Yikes," said Gavin as he got into his own car. "Stay strong."

Gavin made a cross with his fingers, as if Sienna was a vampire.

Will slid in beside Sienna, placing his backpack on the empty center seat between them. "Hey," he said.

"Hey."

Greetings complete, Will looked out the window.

"Sorry for the change of plans, Will," said Stephanie. "Your dad had a work call that ran late. We were nearby, so I told him that I'd pick you up."

Will nodded. When his mom died, Sienna was one of the few people he could stand to be around. Her death had ripped a hole in Sienna's life, too. There was a Stephanie before. And a Stephanie after. Sienna's dad wasn't in the picture, so in her own way, Sienna understood the pain of knowing that nothing would ever be completely okay again.

But as the years passed, it got harder and harder

for Will and Sienna to remain friends. In fourth grade, and definitely by fifth, the gaze of other kids began to sink a little deeper. Will could no longer choose Sienna to walk him to the nurse when he cut his knee at recess. Sienna could no longer borrow Will's recorder when she forgot hers at home.

Outside of school they could still hang out. When their parents got together for dinner, they could have epic video-game battles and gorge on the world's greatest candy salads, which they made by unwrapping all their sugary favorites and tossing them in a mixing bowl.

Although now, in seventh grade, it had been over a year since they'd done anything like that. Will rarely spent more than a last-minute car ride with Sienna. She mostly ignored him at school, and when Will and his dad were invited over for dinner, there was a good chance that Sienna wouldn't be there, ditching at the last minute for Cora's or Audrey's house.

"Trust me, it's better this way," Stephanie would say to Will's dad when he remarked that it was too bad that Sienna couldn't make it. Although part of Will agreed—dinner *was* way smoother without Sienna around complaining about how long the lasagna was taking to bake or the sliminess of the salad dressing— there was a part of Will that missed hanging out with her. When Sienna snorted with laughter or trash-talked his gaming skills, Will could just *be* in a way that he couldn't with anyone else.

So Will was hopeful when Sienna put her phone down. She was the only person who knew how much he hated the *Dr. Dad* podcast. Maybe she would turn to him and acknowledge how annoying it was that his dad had prioritized a work call over picking him up from climbing.

Instead, Sienna asked, "What's the Spanish homework tonight?"

Will shrugged.

"Well, can you check? I think I wrote it down wrong. Señor talks so fast. I can never tell if he's saying thirteen or fourteen."

"*He* talks fast?" said Stephanie from the front seat. "Maybe if you asked Will slowly and added a 'please' to your request, he might be more inclined to help. You can't blame everything on your teachers, Sienna. You wore out that excuse last year with math. Remember?"

Sienna stuck out her tongue. Stephanie didn't notice.

Stephanie was like two sides of a coin. With Will, she was soft and kind. With Sienna, she was hard and cold.

Would his mom be the same way if she were still alive? Would she have a particular tone of voice that she used just with Will? A disappointed glance that she reserved only for him?

It hurt too much to think about.

Will opened his backpack. He took out his math worksheet and his tattered copy of *Roll of Thunder, Hear My Cry*, trying to find his Spanish folder.

"Wait," gasped Sienna, twisting in her seat and straining the seat belt. "Is that Lily's water bottle?"

Ugh.

Will shook his head. "What? No."

Sienna pulled open the flap of Will's backpack. "Right there. That's Lily's. Why do *you* have it?"

There was no way Will could tell Sienna the truth— that he'd meant to return the water bottle to Lily two days ago, but he'd stopped himself because he didn't want *Sienna* to see him do it.

Will had two choices: deny or lie.

He did the social math with the speed of a calculator.

Denying wouldn't work. The teal color was unique, practically electric. And it had that white sticker on the side. Sienna would just ask Lily about it tomorrow and put the pieces together herself.

Lying was the only option.

"Lily let me borrow it," said Will. "I was . . . thirsty. So she gave it to me."

Sienna bugged out her eyes. "Um, weird."

"You know Lily. She's nice." Then realizing the cheesiness of his words, he added: "Too nice."

"Uh-huh," said Sienna, doubt dripping from each syllable.

"Well, isn't that *nice*," said Stephanie. "Sharing with a classmate in need. What a kind thing to do."

"Way to be subtle, Mom," said Sienna.

"Huh," said Stephanie. "Does that mean you're actually listening to me, Sienna?"

Will looked out the window as their back-and-forth continued. It was nothing new. Will had heard them circle endlessly about Sienna's manners. Her appearance. Her attitude.

He was relieved when Stephanie pulled into an open spot outside Will's building. He thanked her for the ride.

"Anytime, sweetheart. I'm always here if you need me. Love you, Will."

Will didn't respond "Love you, too." After all, Sienna was right there. He didn't need to give her another reason to roll her eyes in disgust.

5. Lily

Dinner dropped onto the kitchen counter with a thud. Lily's dad began lifting cartons of Chinese food from a paper bag while simultaneously swatting Lily's hand whenever she tried to reach inside and steal a fortune cookie.

"Don't turn on me, Lil," said her dad. "I can't take two of you."

Lily waited until both his hands were occupied with the lid of a moo shu chicken container and then grabbed a cookie. As Lily unwrapped it, Reese's voice carried into the kitchen.

"You think you know everything, Mom," screamed Reese. "But you don't get it. Just because it doesn't matter to you doesn't mean it's stupid or pointless."

Lily placed the cookie back on the counter. Her

dad sighed and slid it toward her. "It's going to be another one of those joyful family dinners," he said. "Better fuel up."

Lily crunched the cookie between her teeth as she listened to her mom and Reese have the exact same fight they'd been having at least twice a week for months. Their mom believed in school and privacy. Reese believed in fashion and sharing. Their mom wanted Reese to spend more time studying because she was applying to college next year. Reese wanted to build her ReesesPieces Instagram account because she was applying for a summer job with a digital media company that specialized in fashion. Their mom thought social media was a brain-rotting waste of time. Reese thought it was the future.

Lily didn't know who was right and who was wrong. She mostly just wanted the yelling to stop.

A door slammed. Lily's dad shook his head and asked, "When are those two going to realize that they're the exact same person?" He said it quietly, like he was talking to the wonton soup instead of Lily. If he'd wanted an answer, Lily would have said *probably never*. Her mom and sister were both determined, loud, and smart. They were a matching pair of cymbals that kept crashing against each other. Even if their mom didn't think ReesesPieces was important, Lily knew how hard Reese worked on it—laying out her favorite outfits, photographing them against different backgrounds, tagging every brand, and responding to every comment. She had so many followers. Even Sienna!

Which prompted Lily to check her phone. Still no text from Sienna. Disappointed, she joined her family at the table. After a tense dinner (where the subjects of influencers and SAT prep classes were mutually forbidden), Reese went upstairs to her room. Lily helped load the dishwasher and then followed. She knocked on Reese's bedroom door. "It's me."

"Sorry about earlier," said Reese as she let Lily inside. "I just lose it sometimes with Mom. She doesn't get us. She's just, like . . . ARGH!"

Lily loved it when Reese lumped them together as a sisterly unit. There had been a string of years when Reese was twelve, thirteen, and fourteen and

Lily was eight, nine, and ten that Reese had treated her like a bothersome pest. Back then, it seemed to Lily that everything important about Reese's life was stored inside her phone, locked away and password-protected in a place that Lily could never access, no matter how desperately she longed to know what Reese was typing, reading, and laughing about. Or, sometimes, crying over.

Then Lily turned twelve and got her own phone. The wall that Reese had put up between them started to get holes. More and more specks of Reese's life shone through. Even though Lily's phone was super locked-down—she was only allowed five minutes of Instagram per day—she always spent most of her time on ReesesPieces, admiring her sister's eye for fashion and reading all the comments. And Reese usually let Lily scroll through her own phone when her time ran out.

But that night, when Lily plopped down on Reese's leopard-print beanbag chair, she didn't ask to borrow Reese's phone. It had been two days since Maddie had told Lily about Bex, and she hadn't brought it up again. Sienna had been equally silent. On Monday, Lily's life had been set to change, and now it was at a standstill. Was that normal? Reese would know.

"So . . . can I ask you something?" said Lily.

Reese nodded at the chemistry assignment on her screen. "Does it have anything to do with molecules?" Lily shook her head, and Reese closed her laptop. "Then yes, please. Talk as long as you'd like."

"It's about friends. Two different friends, actually." Was it fair to call Sienna a friend? Probably not, but Lily would get to that part.

"Okay, friendship," said Reese. "One of my all-time favorite topics. What did Maddie do this time?"

Lily squinted in surprise. "How did you know I wanted to talk about Maddie?" She'd been planning on starting with Sienna.

Reese stuck out her lower lip, considering. "Well, Maddie's always been the troublemaker in your group. But I love that about her. I really do."

In third and fourth grade, it was true that Maddie would say things to Lily that would cause Lily to collapse in tears as soon as she got home. Little comments about the metallic streamers on her bike looking babyish, or the dirt under her fingernails being disgusting. Even if Lily tried to keep her hurt feelings inside, she usually couldn't last past dinner. And by bedtime? Forget it. She would be curled up on her mom's lap, a blubbering mess.

Now, the urge to share was different, but just as strong. Lily took a deep breath. "Maddie's gay. Or maybe she's bi, I'm not totally sure, but she definitely has a crush on a girl from camp named Bex. And I'm the only one who knows. Except Bex knows. Duh. They text all the time. They agreed that they like each other."

"Okay," said Reese, joining Lily on the floor and crossing her legs. "This is not what I was expecting."

"And it's fine," continued Lily. "I mean, of course it is. I'm happy for her and Bex, even if Bex is amazing at calligraphy, which is supposed to be *my* thing." Reese nodded, biting back a smile. "But . . ."

". . . it's different," said Reese, filling in the silence.

Lily nodded.

". . . and new."

Lily nodded again.

"And different and new is hard."

Now tears leaked from Lily's eyes. She wiped her cheek on the plush beanbag.

Reese ran her fingers through the ends of Lily's hair. "Listen, seventh grade is tricky, Lil. You made it through the emotional roller coaster of sixth grade, which is a huge accomplishment in girl-world, so now you think everything's going to be easier. Because it *should* be easier. And in some ways, it is. But that's only because people are starting to feel more comfortable with who they are. Like Maddie. Maybe she's had crushes on girls before, or maybe this is a totally new thing. Either way, she told *you*. That's a huge compliment."

"A compliment?"

"Of course. You said you're the only one who knows. That means that you're someone Maddie trusts. Maybe more than anyone else."

"I wish she hadn't told only me," whispered Lily. "We're not supposed to keep big secrets from Sasha. It messes everything up."

Reese sighed and opened her arms. "Listen Lil, that's kind of unrealistic. Things are going to keep changing. There's no way to avoid it. And I hate to say this, but it gets even trickier. If not with friends, then with other people. Look at me and Mom. I'm old enough to know who I am and what I want, but I still have to fight for it."

As Lily leaned into her sister, she wondered if Reese was correct. She almost told Reese the next part—that it wasn't just the secret of Maddie liking a girl that was hard. It was that Maddie suddenly had so many things that Lily couldn't figure out. She had a crush on someone who had a crush on her back. She had a sport that she loved and a best friend to play that sport with. Maddie had even been on Sienna's list for dates to the dance. Sienna was going to pair her with Theo!

In every single way, Lily was falling behind. But before she could put that into words, her phone pinged with a new text.

"That's probably Maddie now," said Reese. "I bet she's sending viral puppy videos, like all good friends do."

Lily smiled and picked up her phone. It wasn't Maddie. It was from a number she didn't recognize, with just one word:

Hey

Then a few seconds later.

It's Will
From school

"Was I right?" asked Reese.

Lily shook her head. "It's not Maddie. It's a boy."

"See!" said Reese. "Constantly changing! Just like your wise older sister predicted."

"What do I do?"

"Well, is he cute?"

Will wasn't in her saved list of contacts, so there was no photo to share. And he wasn't easy to describe, with his shaggy hair, well-worn T-shirts, and thick eyelashes. But yes, he was definitely cute. Lily looked up at Reese and nodded. "Yeah. Kind of."

"Then you text him back, silly. Go forth and flirt. I'm always here if you need me."

Lily hesitated. But when Reese nodded toward the bedroom door, Lily threw her head back and said, "Fine. But for the record, I'm not going to flirt. I'm just going to text back the normal way."

"Funny," said Reese, "I don't think your cheeks are *normally* so rosy."

Lily brought her hands to her face. Her cheeks were a little warm. She turned away before Reese noticed that she was also fighting back a smile.

6. Will

Will sat on his bed, the teal water bottle with the STRONG IS THE NEW PRETTY sticker next to him, and waited for Lily to respond.

What had he been thinking?

Lily didn't even talk to him at school.

What would Will think if a random "Hey" had popped up on his screen?

Wrong number, that's what. Which was why he'd added "From school." To be clear. And safe.

At first Will wasn't sure he even had Lily's number. He'd had to search through one of the huge group texts from the end of sixth grade when Sienna had interpreted Ms. Follstrom's lessons about inclusivity to mean that she should collect the numbers of everyone who had a cell phone and start a grade-wide group chat.

For weeks, Will's phone had buzzed with messages like:

This is me

                    Me who?

Emma

                    Which Emma?

It was a massive failure. Although, when Gavin started welcoming every new addition as if he was a British lord—"Welcome, kind sir" and "Top of the morning, madam"—it had gotten a lot funnier.

Will remembered that Lily had added a flower emoji next to her name. At the time he'd thought that was a nice touch. Now it made finding her number a little easier.

But starting a new text to just Lily? That was not easy at all.

Except what choice did he have? Sienna had seen Lily's water bottle in his backpack. When it came to information like that, it didn't matter that he and Sienna used to be close friends, or were still sometimes friends, or whatever confusing thing they were.

If Will didn't clear things up, it was only a matter of time before they spilled into a Sienna-shaped mess. The kind that left a stain no matter how hard you tried to scrub it clean.

Suddenly his phone pinged with a reply text from Lily.

Hey

Shoot. Now what? His heart racing, Will typed the only thing he could think of—an emoji of a hand waving hello.

Seriously? Couldn't he even type actual words? Like: *I picked up your water bottle after lunch on Monday. Just wanted you to know in case you were looking for it. I'll bring it to school tomorrow.*

But before Will could write anything close to that, Lily texted again:

What's up?

Will could feel her on the other side of his phone wondering what was going on. Maybe she was texting Maddie and Sasha in between responding to him. Asking their advice.

It was time to start making some sense. Will typed:

I found your water bottle

Oh. Thx. I was looking
for it

No prob

Can u bring it to school?

K

Thx!

That was it. Totally blah. As if Lily was texting a brick wall. The kind of text chain that even Will's dad couldn't spin into a podcast episode.

Will held his phone for another minute in case Lily sent something more. When it remained silent, he tossed it into the center of his bed next to his unfinished homework.

Ice cream. Will needed ice cream.

He walked down the hall into the kitchen, where his dad was sitting at the counter in front of his laptop. His hands were clasped behind his head, and he was looking at the ceiling as if he had just let out a long exhale.

His dad wasn't fuming mad, but he wasn't happy. There was a strong hint of disappointment in the way his lower lip curled down.

Will almost turned back to his room. But a creaky floorboard gave him away.

"Ah," said his dad, releasing his hands. "Just the man I wanted to see."

Will kept moving toward the freezer. If he was going to get a lecture, he might as well top it off with something tasty.

"Do you know who just emailed me?" asked his dad.

"Oprah?" said Will.

It was a running inside joke ever since a parenting website had described the *Dr. Dad* podcast as "Oprah with dad jokes." Oprah was one of his dad's idols, a famous talk-show host turned one-woman media empire. Dad jokes were an equal combination of funny and pitiful. So in Will's opinion, the magazine had pretty much nailed it.

Any mention of Oprah usually made his dad chuckle. But not tonight.

"Nice try," said his dad. "It was actually Mr. Stanlow updating me about an incident at lunch on Monday and some photography assignment. Ring any bells?"

Not cool, thought Will. Mr. Stanlow had said that he wasn't going to email his dad—yet. But what could Will do about it? Nothing.

Will shrugged. Then he scooped a large helping of Oreo cookie fudge into a bowl.

"Care to elaborate?" asked his dad. "In words?"

"Not really."

"Listen, Will . . ." Then came the pause in which his dad thought through all the back episodes of *Dr. Dad.* All the parenting experts and psychologists and celebrities who he'd had on the show, seeking the perfect piece of wisdom to impart to his son.

Will wished someone would tell his dad that the pause was the problem.

All he wanted was for his dad to speak in his own words. Using his own brain. And yes, as cheesy as it was, from his own heart.

Because then maybe it would stay just between them. And Will could talk to him about Gavin and the way it felt not to always like the person who was your closest friend.

He could bring up Lily and how, when he held her teal water bottle, he could feel the warmth of her hands on the hard surface, even though that made no sense at all.

They could discuss the "How I See It" assignment, which was equal parts stupid and intriguing.

And speaking of pictures, maybe Will would attempt to explain how when he looked at framed photographs of him with his mom, he sometimes wanted to punch himself. Because he should have been paying closer attention. Committing her smell and the sensation of her arms to memory.

Then maybe he wouldn't miss her with such an endless, empty ache.

Instead, Will pounded his ice cream and put the

bowl in the dishwasher. "Sorry I screwed up, Dad. I'll try harder next time."

"Thank you, Will. That's all I can ask. So are we good? On the same page?"

"Yeah, Dad. We're good."

A lie. The easy way out. Because just like on the climbing wall, following a familiar path was easier than risking a new route.

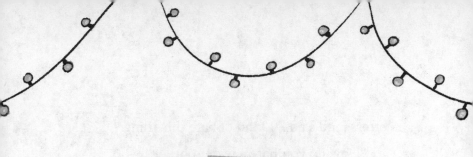

7. Lily

On Thursday morning Lily was stuffing her jacket in a locker when Will appeared. He held her teal water bottle at the end of a stiff arm and said, "Here you go."

"Thanks," said Lily.

"Sorry I didn't give it back to you earlier," he said. "I forgot to bring it yesterday and . . ." His words trailed off, just like they sometimes did in class.

"That's okay. I didn't get thirsty." Lily nodded toward the water dispenser a few feet away. It was supposed to be a joke. Thankfully, Will laughed.

"Phew," he said, wiping his forehead and smiling.

Maybe that explained why Lily glanced down at the water bottle, the words STRONG IS THE NEW PRETTY staring back at her with their bold black letters, and said, "I kind of hate this thing."

"How do you hate a water bottle?"

"Not the water bottle," said Lily. "The sticker. I feel like it's judging me."

Yikes! Why had she said that? Besides the fact that it was the truth. Lily did hate the sticker. She did feel like it was judging her. At the very beginning of the soccer season, Coach Brennan had handed the stickers out to every girl on the school team. "So you never forget what matters," she'd said. Lily had been excited to place the sticker on her water bottle, making sure the top edge was evenly spaced with the rim. But then the season progressed and Lily realized how terrible she was at soccer. Apparently, she was not *strong* enough. Still, this wasn't the sort of thing Lily would normally confess out loud. Especially to Will, who she barely knew.

But then Will tilted his head and said, "That *strong* is kind of judgey. Like, why all the capital letters, buddy? We hear you already."

"Exactly," said Lily. "It's totally judgey. And also, what does it even mean? If you're not pretty, do you have to be strong? What if you're not strong *or* pretty?

Are you nothing? Can't you just be, like, in-between? A lowercase letter kind of person."

"A lowercase letter kind of person," repeated Will. "I like that. It sounds like the name of a band. The Lowercase Letters."

Lily smiled, relieved that Will had lightened the heavy thing that she hadn't intended to say. "Totally," she agreed. "Like a preschool band that takes the stage in tiny leather jackets and shakes maracas."

"I would pay big bucks to see that," said Will.

"Me too."

"Maybe we could be their managers," continued Will. "Drop out of school to start recruiting kids."

Lily laughed. "We could go to those toddler music classes in Rittenhouse Park to scout the talent."

"Hide behind some trees so they don't see us and get all nervous. And, you know . . ." Will mimicked a kid who'd just wet their pants.

"That would not be good."

"Not good at all."

Then Lily said, "They could even play at the school dance."

Will dropped his gaze to the ground. "Yeah. Maybe."

Ugh. Why did she have to mention the dance? It was like tossing a bucket of mud onto their conversation. And it didn't even make sense. There wouldn't be a band at the dance. There would be a DJ. Every single person in school knew that. She'd just had this funny image in her head of toddlers with electric guitars jamming on stage. The words slipped out. Now Lily was desperate to slip away as well.

"Anyway," she said. "Thanks for returning it."

Will nodded. "No problem."

Lily walked down the hall, turning the stupid dance comment over in her mind. What if Will thought she had been trying to send him a hint about asking her to the dance? What if he told Gavin? By the end of the day, Sienna would be writing Will's name next to Lily's at the very bottom of her list. Which wouldn't be terrible, would it? Will was not Theo, or any of Theo's soccer-playing friends, but he was funny. And talking to him was so easy.

Was this how Maddie felt about Bex? Was this the

feeling that had made Maddie's eyes light up when she'd read Bex's text on Monday? Lily had to know and she could not wait until lunch. Her homeroom was on the second floor, but she passed the staircase and kept walking to the section of seventh-grade lockers at the far end of the hall. When she spotted Maddie, Lily reached for her arm. "Emergency," she said.

Maddie smiled. "Good emergency, or bad emergency?"

"Good. I mean, maybe. I don't know. That's part of the emergency."

"Ooooh," said Maddie. "I love those kind."

Homeroom started in five minutes, and the hallway was way too crowded for this conversation. So they stepped inside the empty science lab, standing with their shoulders pressed against the side wall so no one could see them through the door window. With the electric hum of the computer equipment drowning out any outside noise, Lily asked, "You know that thing you told me about Bex?"

Maddie nodded. Her cheeks turned rosy.

"How did you know that you *liked* liked her?" asked Lily.

"You mean since she's a girl?"

Lily shook her head. "I mean in all the ways."

Maddie slid her backpack off her shoulders, resting it at her feet. "At first Bex and I were just friends," she said. "But then I realized that I wanted to be around her all the time. More than anyone else in our cabin. And I wondered if she felt the same way about me because, somehow, we were always together. We chose all the same activities and sat next to each other at meals. We literally spent every single second by each other's sides. And you know how sometimes I can get a little . . . grumpy?"

"Sometimes?" said Lily, laughing.

Maddie smiled. "Well, that never ever happened with Bex. Not even once. The more time we spent together, the more I wanted to tell her all my secrets or whatever." Maddie paused, a mischievous twinkle growing in her eyes. "Is there a reason you're suddenly asking me all these questions, Lil? Please tell me this has nothing to do with Theo."

Theo's name took Lily by surprise. She wasn't comparing Maddie's explanation to the way she thought about Theo; she was comparing it to the way she thought about Will.

"I'm over Theo," said Lily.

Maddie nodded. "Good. Theo's okay and all, but you can do way better."

Just as Lily was about to ask *What do you think about Will?*, Maddie checked the time on her phone and reached for her backpack. "Shoot. Homeroom. See you at lunch?"

"Yeah," said Lily. "Of course."

Maddie ran down the hall and Lily raced up the stairs. The higher Lily climbed, the more her feelings for Will changed from an emergency into a question. Lily didn't know the exact answer, but she was excited to figure it out.

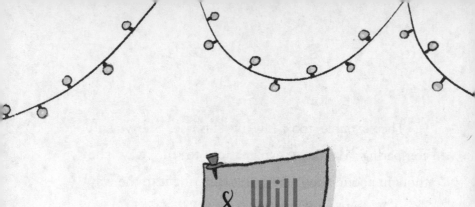

8. Will

When Lily left, her water bottle in her hand, Will had no choice but to walk in the opposite direction. Right past the "How I See It" bulletin board.

So far, four days after being given the camera, Will had taken zero photos. When his dad had asked about his progress on the assignment that morning, Will promised that he'd get started. Otherwise, he'd worried his dad would email Mr. Stanlow.

Apparently those two loved keeping in touch.

As Will looked at the empty board, he regretted not taking a picture of the sticker on Lily's water bottle. He'd thought about explaining the assignment to her, but then she'd brought up the dance and her cheeks turned bright red. She'd scooted away so quickly there'd been no time.

Will kept walking.

Suddenly Sienna appeared beside him, breathless with joy. "Did I just see what I think I saw? You and *Lily*?"

Uh-oh.

On the climbing wall, one of Will's favorite holds was the side pull; a vertical hold shaped like a half moon. To keep their balance, climbers leaned away from side pulls before launching themselves upward. In moments like this, when Sienna was all revved up and actually speaking to him in public, she was like a human side pull.

To remain steady, Will had to lean away.

"No," he answered.

Sienna shook her head. "Nice try. You can't fool me, Will. I know you have a crush on Lily. I can see it deep in your eyes."

It took every ounce of hard-earned muscle control to keep his eyelids open, his eyeballs steady.

"Shut up," he hissed.

Sienna clapped her hands. "OMG, I knew it! As soon as I saw her water bottle in your backpack yesterday, I sensed that something was up. You should have told me sooner. I can totally help you." She brought her finger to her jaw, imitating a thinker's pose. "According to my records, Lily doesn't have a date to the dance and neither do you. It's meant to be! Do you want me to ask her for you? I can do that. It would be my greatest honor."

"Stay out of it," warned Will.

Sienna lifted her hands defensively. "Geez, chill out, Will. I'm just trying to help."

"I don't need your help."

"Fine. Whatever. Do it your own way. But you know where to find me when you realize that you actually *do* need me. I just hope it's not too late." Sienna waved goodbye. Her fingers flitted in the air.

Deep inside, frustration boiled.

Will threw his backpack to the ground and pulled his Power Putty from the front pocket.

Working his fingers deeper and deeper distracted Will from the truth.

He *did* like Lily. In that way.

He liked how she had so many thoughts spinning

inside her. The way she blushed when one escaped that she'd meant to keep hidden.

The crinkle of her eyes.

How her voice grew louder the longer she spoke in class. The way she paused when she needed to sort out an idea, but then kept going.

He liked how she had Maddie and Sasha, but how she sometimes seemed separate. In their circle, but a little off-center, toward the edge.

Except what was Will supposed to do about these feelings beside knead them into his putty?

He wasn't going to the dance. The story of Will's first middle school dance would make an excellent *Dr. Dad* episode. He couldn't give his dad the satisfaction.

There had to be another way.

Suddenly Sienna stopped walking. She turned back toward him. There was a softness in her eyes, a hint of the old Sienna. The one he used to spend so much time with.

She parted her lips, as if she was maybe going to apologize for being so pushy about Lily. But then Cora appeared. She bumped her hip against Sienna's.

Cora followed Sienna's gaze. Right toward Will.

They whispered something that Will did not need to hear to understand. Sienna resumed walking, in step with Cora.

Maybe it was the missed opportunity to photograph the sticker. Or maybe they were the perfect summation of how he actually saw school. The right girls at the right time.

Either way, Will pulled the camera from his backpack and took his very first Polaroid.

The picture dropped from the device into his hand, the image slowly coming into focus. Sienna and Cora. Their heads tilted toward each other. Their legs in sync.

Telling secrets. Stirring up trouble.

The picture didn't change anything. They hadn't heard the click of the shutter, or the gentle whirr of the rollers.

But something about pressing the button reminded Will of hitting the buzzer at the top of the climbing wall. It was the satisfaction of completing an act.

And with it came a flick of power.

9. Lily

On Friday, Maddie and Sasha had an early dismissal for a soccer game. Lily was walking toward the library, where she was planning to spend her afternoon free period and maybe get a book to keep her company over the weekend, when Sienna called out for her to wait up.

"Hey, Lily," said Sienna. "What are you up to tonight?"

Sienna spoke in her easy breezy way, but the question knocked Lily off-balance. Before she could think through the embarrassment factor of her answer, Lily said, "Oh, uh, nothing."

"Cool," said Sienna. "Want to sleep over at my house?"

Lily was shocked. Sienna still hadn't texted her

the evil-eye necklace link or anything else, and she'd never once invited Lily over to her house. Plus, a sleepover was way different than just hanging out. It was a lot of time. But Lily had nothing else to do and, more than that, she was flattered. Maybe Sienna did want to be friends after all.

"Sure," said Lily. "I'd love to."

"Perfect! How about come over at six?" Then Sienna turned, as if nothing major had just happened, and walked away.

Lily checked the time. It was one thirty. Six o'clock wasn't that far away, but the gulf between now and then widened with every passing second and every new question. Why was Sienna inviting her to sleep over? Which pajamas should she pack? Would Sienna step out of the room while Lily changed? Or would they change together? In which case, Lily had to remember to wear a bra even though she'd forgotten to wear one to school. Should she bring her retainer? Or would Sienna notice the slimy film that had recently collected around the edges of the case and be grossed out? Was Sienna like Maddie, who got cranky when she was tired? Or was she like Sasha, who got sillier and louder as the night got later?

By the time Lily reached the entrance to the library, her mind and heart were racing double speed. She waited until the librarian was out of sight, then hid her phone under the table and texted the group chat:

Sleeping over at Sienna's tonight

So random!

Sasha responded first:

OMG what if she kills with you with her death stare!
I don't want you to die!

Then Maddie:

Do not go to sleep

Do not close your eyes

Maybe eat some garlic?

Sasha, a minute later:

Sorry

Had to explain to Maddie

how death stares work

Maddie:

Whatever

I get it now

Just don't die Lily

You're too young!

Sasha:

And beautiful!

Even though the texts made Lily laugh, she couldn't ignore the image of Maddie and Sasha in the backseat of the car, talking back and forth as they wrote. If the sleepover was a success and she became friends with Sienna, would Maddie and Sasha be jealous? Lily hoped so. It was their turn to understand how it felt.

That evening Lily and her mom walked the five blocks to Sienna's building. They didn't fight the way Reese and her mom fought, but Lily was increasingly aware of what she shared with her mom and how she shared it. Like with the sleepover. Lily had presented it as full-on exciting, when it was actually also a little confusing.

So Lily was surprised when her mom stopped her right as they were about to cross the street. "Are you sure about this, Lily?" asked her mom. "Because you can always change your mind. Or blame me. Tell Sienna that there was some kind of family emergency. I'm here to take the fall for whatever you need."

"Of course I'm sure," lied Lily. "It's just a sleepover."

"A sleepover with *Sienna*."

"What's wrong with Sienna?"

Her mom tilted her face toward the sky, a how-should-I-say-this look in her eyes. "Sienna's never struck me as being the kindest girl in your grade. Remember when I volunteered at school for the Egyptian pyramid craft? She barely had the patience to count out sugar cubes, let alone help her group stack them."

"Wow," said Lily. "Way to hold fourth grade against her, Mom."

"Honey, some personality traits never change."

"And some do. You don't even know her."

Her mom sighed. "And neither do you, Lil."

Whatever, thought Lily. Sienna was a stylish, outgoing, people person. Like Reese. Not like their mom, who was cautious and skeptical, her lips pressed tight with concern. When the light turned, Lily took a step ahead. She couldn't explain the choice she was making—to be more like Sienna, more like Reese—without hurting her mom's feelings. So she kept walking. By the time Lily stepped out of the elevator on the fifteenth floor of Sienna's building, she was ready.

"Hey," said Sienna. "You're right on time."

Lily smiled and followed Sienna down a long hallway until they reached the apartment at the very end. Sienna's mom was sitting at the kitchen counter, a home décor magazine open in front of her.

"Mom, this is Lily. See. She's very nice. Just like I told you."

Lily stood, her overnight bag still on her shoulder, trying to look nice. Thankfully, Sienna's mom didn't seem to need any convincing. She stood and wrapped Lily in a tight hug.

"Oh, Lily. We're so happy you're here. I'm thrilled. Just thrilled. Maybe we'll make some ice cream sundaes later?"

Sienna rolled her eyes and pulled on Lily's arm, guiding her farther into the apartment until they reached Sienna's closed bedroom door. Lily had seen snippets of Sienna's room over Zoom during remote schooling, so she had some idea what to expect. But the reality of stepping inside was still shocking. The walls were a crisp white with massive black-painted stars. There were chains of neon-colored felt pom-

pom balls draped around the moldings. The full-length mirror was decorated with celebrity photos and stickers. The other bedrooms that Lily knew well—her own, Maddie's, and Sasha's—seemed so immature in comparison. Like they belonged to little girls who still wore tutus and princess dresses.

Sienna picked up a light pink bottle that was decorated with gold letters and sprayed it into the air, filling the room with the sweet smell of roses. Then she sat down on her bed.

"I love your perfume," said Lily as she placed her sleepover bag near the door.

"Not perfume," corrected Sienna. "Room spray."

Lily blushed. "Right. That's what I meant."

Sienna shrugged, as if it was no big deal. But the mistake lingered in the air like the scent itself.

"I actually love your whole room," said Lily, trying again.

"It's okay," said Sienna. "I'm getting kind of tired of it. I might change it up soon."

Lily nodded in agreement, although she wondered how any room could be preferable to this one.

Thankfully, Sienna broke the awkward silence. "Can I ask you something? Do you think I should go to the dance with Jake?"

Sasha's former crush. The one who had spent the summer flipping off lifeguards and stealing from the pool snack bar. He and Sienna were both popular, even though Jake's popularity was what allowed him to get away with being a doofus. Did Sienna know that Sasha had a crush on him? Was this some kind of test?

"I don't know . . ." stalled Lily. "Do you have his number?"

"Duh."

"Is he nice over text? Or is he . . ." Lily wasn't sure how to say *as stupid as he is in real life* without offending Sienna. What if she really liked him? Lily sat next to Sienna on her bed. Sienna's phone was resting between them, ready and waiting. Lily expected Sienna to pick it up and maybe show her one of their text chains. Instead, Sienna smiled and said, "What about Will?"

Lily's body temperature rose. "Will?"

Sienna nodded. "Do *you* guys text?"

Lily shook her head. They'd only ever texted about the water bottle, which was not in the way Sienna meant.

"Huh," said Sienna. "That's surprising. Because Will has a crush on you. Obviously."

"No, he doesn't."

"He does. Trust me. I've known Will since we were babies. Our moms were best friends." Sienna paused, seeming to shake off a thought. Then she continued: "Honestly, you two would be perfect together. The dance is next weekend, and I think you should go with him. If I decide to go with Jake, we could all meet up or something."

The words spritzed out of Sienna's mouth like the room spray. They were supposed to land on Lily's skin and transform her into a girl who smelled like roses and casually texted with a boy who had a crush on her. Instead, Lily's mind raced. Was it just a coincidence that Sienna thought she and Will were a match? Or had Lily unknowingly dropped a hint that she was curious about Will?

"Don't be a chicken," said Sienna as Lily hesitated. "Just text him. I would never give you bad advice."

Sienna walked over to her desk where a silver jewelry holder in the shape of a tree displayed a large collection of necklaces, rings, and bracelets. She gathered the chains of the necklaces, sifting through them until the different-sized pendants lay in her cupped palm. Then she chose one and lifted it from the tree. "Here. Wear this. It will protect you."

It was the evil-eye necklace with the turquoise center stone that Lily had admired in the Secret Coffee Shop. Sienna placed it in Lily's hand. It was lighter than Lily expected and cool to the touch. The tiny diamonds in the corners of the eye sparkled as the chain slinked to the lowest point of her cupped palm.

Lily couldn't resist. She walked to the mirror and fastened the necklace around her neck.

Suddenly she understood. It wasn't the diamonds or the swirl of the turquoise stone that made the necklace so perfect, so special. It was the way the sleek evil eye fell against her collarbone. She looked older and confident. Trendy, even. Like how she felt when Reese styled her for ReesesPieces.

"I love it," said Lily, placing her hand against the pendant.

"Just so we're clear," said Sienna, "I'm not giving it to you. I'm lending you its protective power. You know, since it's an evil eye, nothing bad can happen when you're wearing it."

Lily blinked, the spell of her reflection broken. "Right. Totally."

"So come on," said Sienna. "Text Will. Start with something casual and flirty. Maybe bring up the puppies on Mr. Myron's socks. Puppies always get people in the mood."

If Sienna had been Maddie or Sasha, Lily would have cracked up over "in the mood." It was super cringey. There would have been pillows tossed at heads and exaggerated sounds of barfing. But with Sienna, Lily kept a straight face.

"I don't know."

"Come on, Lily. Don't be such a baby."

Lily looked at her phone, which she'd set down on Sienna's desk. She *should* just text Will. It was so not a big deal. Then Sienna would be happy and the rest of the sleepover would go smoothly. Maybe Sienna would want to sleep over at her house next time. Lily would have to up the coolness factor of her room, but Reese could help with that.

Except when Lily opened her texts, her thumb froze over the screen. Sienna would see that she and Will already had a text chain. She'd probably force Lily to let her read it. The texts were boring and innocent, but still. Sienna would sprinkle the words with meanings they didn't have and blow it up into something bigger. Will might never talk to her again.

"I can't," said Lily. "I don't want to embarrass him."

"I already told you that he likes you," said Sienna. "You won't embarrass him. You'll, like, make his night. And Will's not even cool. It doesn't matter. Just do it."

As impatience boiled in Sienna's eyes, Lily debated the meaning of Sienna's words. If Will *was* cool, if he was Theo or Jake, it would matter? And if Sienna thought she and Will were perfect for each other, that meant she thought they were social equals. But Will was an outsider. A hoodie sweatshirt loner with just

Gavin as a friend. If that's how Sienna thought of Lily, too, why was Lily even sleeping over? Suddenly the entire night seemed like some kind of joke with Lily, or maybe even Will, as the punch line.

"I can't," said Lily.

Sienna exhaled with disgust. "Fine. So what do you think we should do all night, eat ice sundaes with my *mom*? No way. If you're not going to be any fun, then maybe you should go home early. Like right now. This sleepover is canceled."

10. Will

Will and Gavin had a Friday night/Saturday morning routine.

On Friday night they slept at Gavin's house. On Saturday morning Will's dad picked them up and took them to open climb at Philly Rocks.

It worked. As in, it didn't *not* work. Gavin's mom was super lax about screen time, so they usually stayed up until at least midnight. Gavin worked on his YouTube channel while Will watched climbing videos on Gavin's phone. The phone's case had a nick in its side that Will suspected was from the lunch incident. But neither of them mentioned it.

Thankfully, Gavin was done with old ladies slamming telephones against walls and had moved on to 1980s time travel movies spliced with clips from luxury car advertisements. The videos were equally stupid and nonsensical as his old ones, but at least they had nothing to do with Will or *Dr. Dad*. For now.

"It's missing the magic sauce," murmured Gavin as he reviewed his latest edit.

"Maybe you need to swipe some of Stanlow's sriracha," joked Will. "Sprinkle it on top."

Gavin laughed. "That stuff is golden. I could chug a whole bottle of it no problem."

No you couldn't, thought Will. *You would barf your guts out*. Instead of saying that, however, he leaned over and told Gavin to show him what he had so far.

"It's from *Back to the Future*," explained Gavin. "The part where Marty McFly's dad is in a tree peeping on Marty's hot young mom."

Gavin hit Play. A teenage boy was balanced on a tree limb, spying on a girl in a bra. Marty McFly rode up on his bicycle and surprised the peeper, who fell from the tree and sprinted away right in time for Marty to get hit by a passing car. As the driver yelled, "Another one of those damn kids jumped in front of my car," Gavin cut to a clip of a silver Porsche racing down a mountainside road.

Will laughed. "McFly never stood a chance against that thing."

Gavin squinted. "You actually like it?"

"Yeah," said Will. "It's hilarious."

"Huh. Didn't see that coming."

"You mean McFly and the car?"

"No," said Gavin. "I mean you actually liking one of my clips."

"I like your clips."

Gavin huffed and clasped both hands to his heart. "Wow, dude. Don't make me cry with your outpouring of emotion."

"Whatever," said Will. "I'm going to sleep."

Will laid down on Gavin's extra bed and pulled the comforter to his chin. As Gavin continued to work, the pounding of computer keys oddly rhythmic and soothing, Will wondered if maybe it was time to be a little nicer. Or more expressive. Or something.

The next morning, however, as they ate blueberry muffins while Gavin's little sister played with her bubble-eyed miniature dolls and Gavin hypothesized about doll deaths, the familiar itch to flee Gavin's company returned.

As soon as his dad rounded the corner of Gavin's block, Will jumped up from the window seat where he was keeping watch for his arrival.

Gavin followed. The routine, after all, was set.

When Will was alone with his dad, he sat in the front seat. But when Gavin was there, he sat in the back. Otherwise, Gavin would make a big deal about calling shotgun even though it was Will's car.

Some things just weren't worth dealing with.

As soon as they piled in, their bags in the trunk, his dad's phone rang through the Bluetooth with a call from Stephanie.

Will caught Gavin's eye, signaling for him to stay quiet. Sometimes when his dad was driving *and* talking, he forgot that he was on speakerphone. And Stephanie rarely called this early in the morning. There was a good chance that something interesting was up.

"Hey, Steph," said his dad.

"You are never going to believe what Sienna did last night," said Stephanie.

Gavin flared his eyes and nibbled on his fingertips. Will had to hunch over to keep from laughing. Gavin had hilarious facial expressions.

"Okay," said his dad. "Try me."

"So she'd invited this new girl over to sleep over," continued Stephanie. "Not *new* new, but new to me. Her name's Lily? Maybe you know her. She's been in their grade forever. Anyway. Super-sweet girl. So of course I'm thrilled, because you and I both know that Sienna could use some sweet girls in her life. I mean, we've talked about that. How she needs some nicer friends."

Gavin sunk down in his seat, as if trying to shrink himself in order to increase the chances of the conversation continuing to play on speakerphone. While Will understood the impulse, part of him wanted to clear his throat. Cough. Kick the back of his dad's seat.

Anything to jolt his dad into stopping the call.

Sienna invited Lily to a sleepover? Not good.

But Will stayed silent and still as the conversation continued.

"I know Lily," said his dad. "Yes, sweet girl."

"Exactly," said Stephanie. "So I'm thrilled. Letting them do their own thing. Blah, blah, blah. And then suddenly, out of nowhere, Sienna comes barreling out of her room and announces that the sleepover is over."

"Over?"

"Yep. She just declares it like she's the boss. And when I try to ask what happened, Sienna just says that Lily wants to go home. Which, fine, okay. Maybe the girl's homesick. I mean, they're in seventh grade, but still. To each their own, right? But when Lily comes out of Sienna's room, it is clear—clear as day—that something happened. I'm telling you, Rob, this girl's face. She was shocked."

Will's dad began to speak, but Stephanie cut him off. "What am I supposed to do now, huh? Sienna swears that nothing happened. That Lily just changed her mind about sleeping over. But I don't buy it. You know Sienna, she's a handful and sometimes she can be . . ."

Stephanie's voice trailed off, as if searching for the appropriate word. Will had no trouble whatsoever. He whispered the word "evil" to Gavin.

That did it. Gavin spewed a mouthful of laughter and spit.

"Oh crap," said Will's dad, glancing in the rearview mirror. "Steph, I can't talk right now. I'll call you back."

He ended the call and pulled into an open parking spot on the side of the road. Taking off his seat belt, he turned to face them and said, "Gentleman, you did not hear that."

Gavin shook his head. "Didn't hear a thing. Not even a little bit. No, sir."

"Will?"

"Same. Not one single word."

"Okay, good." Will's dad paused, searching for the perfect parenting advice. "Because while it would be understandable for you to be curious, that conversation was intended for grown-ups. Sometimes adults make mistakes, just like kids."

"We get it, Dad."

"Loud and clear," agreed Gavin, with a hand salute.

As his dad fiddled with the console screen, probably double-checking that the call was disconnected, Will looked out the window.

Were Sienna and Lily friends all of a sudden? No way. Not a chance. Sienna had Cora and Audrey. Lily had Maddie and Sasha. Totally different crews.

So why did Sienna invite Lily to sleep over? And why did Lily agree to go?

Gavin nudged Will in the shoulder. Then he hissed and made the motion of a cat.

Cat fight. The term they sometimes used to refer to girls fighting.

Oh man. Now Gavin had done it.

Will's dad whipped his head around.

"No way, Gavin. We don't discount the emotions of girls by reducing them to gendered stereotypes. Not in this car. Got it?"

This time Gavin merely nodded. No words. No hand salutes.

Will bit back a smile of pride. His dad could be a full-on *dad*, but he also had moments of coolness. And for once, someone had succeeded in shutting Gavin up.

Although, it didn't last long.

Despite staying silent for the remainder of the car ride, Gavin was not giving up his fight theory. In the Philly Rocks locker room he acted out both sides of the imaginary fight, declaring Sienna the hands-down winner.

Will didn't laugh. But he also didn't stop the stupid production. His dad would have, just like in the car. But his dad was forty-five, not thirteen.

Big difference.

And also, it was harmless because Gavin was obviously wrong. Sienna was not physical. Her weapons were words. Will wasn't sure exactly how Lily would match up, but he was certain that it hadn't been a fair fight.

He should text Lily.

He should totally text her.

He totally wanted to text her.

But the evidence of what had happened last time was right there, glowing on his screen. Definitely not a rejection. But also not an invitation to try again.

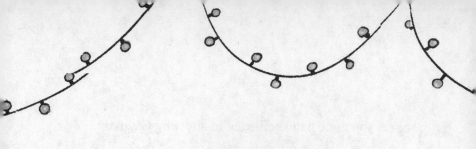

11. Lily

Lily laid the evil-eye necklace on her desk, running her fingers along the silver chain so that all the links were flat. The sleepover had ended so abruptly—so dramatically—that neither Lily nor Sienna had remembered that Lily was still wearing the necklace when she took the elevator downstairs to the lobby, barely making it out of the building's revolving front doors before collapsing into her mom's arms, tears streaming down her cheeks. The pendant must have slipped inside the neckline of her shirt as she walked home and then spent the rest of the terrible night watching TV with her parents. It was only when Lily changed into her pajamas, pulling a fresh pair from her dresser drawer because she couldn't bear to wear the ones she'd chosen for the sleepover, that she noticed the evil eye against her clavicle.

Now it was Sunday evening. So far Lily had moved the necklace from her desk drawer to her underwear drawer to the inside zipped pocket of her backpack and back to her desk. Obviously she had to return the necklace to Sienna. Even though Sienna had that whole tree full of jewelry, she'd eventually notice the evil eye was missing. But the idea of handing the necklace to Sienna—with what? An apology? Remorse?—was impossible.

As her parents called up a bedtime warning, Lily found a white envelope and placed the necklace inside. Using a blue pen, Lily wrote Sienna's name as plainly as possible. Even so, the smooth S and the flowing bumps of the two lowercase n's still looked great. At the last minute, Lily added one of her signature flowers to the end of Sienna's name. The extra touch was possibly pathetic, but maybe it would remind Sienna that Lily was nice. It was worth a shot. Tomorrow morning Lily would go straight to Sienna's locker, slide the envelope with the necklace inside between the slats, and never think about it again.

Just as Lily sealed the envelope shut, her bedroom door opened and Reese stepped inside. "Mom ordered me to tell you that it's time for bed," said Reese. "Not that I care. Just earning some good daughter points by relaying the message."

Without quite understanding why, Lily turned the envelope over. But not fast enough to escape Reese's notice.

"What are you hiding, Lil?" asked Reese. "Don't tell me you're suddenly competing for the role of bad daughter."

"It's nothing."

Reese pursed her lips. Of course she could sense that the envelope was *something*. Reese spent hours poring over tiny digital squares, searching for messages in the way a belt was placed in a waistband or a blanket was tossed on a bed. Objects could send signals—of coolness, of confidence, of control—and Lily's flipped envelope was just the opposite.

"Is it a love letter?" asked Reese. "Is that boy from school so obsessed with you that he's moved on from texting to actually writing words on paper?"

Lily shook her head, but the reference to Will brought a smile to her lips. Reese jumped onto Lily's bed, lying sideways. "Okay," she continued. "So not a love letter. Figures. Romance is so dead these days." Reese shrugged. "Well, that's my only guess. You're just going to have to tell me what you're hiding because Mom took my phone away until I start on her stupid SAT flash cards. I've got nothing but time."

A wave of relief washed over Lily. She'd wanted to talk to Reese about Sienna ever since the afternoon in the Secret Coffee Shop. And even more so since the sleepover. But Reese was always out with friends, or distracted with ReesesPieces and applying to summer internships, and there was never an opening for Lily to tap her big sister on the shoulder and say something incredibly pathetic like *the most popular girl in seventh grade kicked me out of our sleepover*. Now, with the city lights twinkling outside her bedroom window, Lily told Reese everything.

"So basically," said Reese when Lily finished, "you stood up for yourself, that pissed Sienna off, and she threw a temper tantrum."

It sounded so simple. And also, true. In the moment, however, Lily had felt like Sienna was the mature one and she was the baby. Reese's take was way better, but what was Lily supposed to do about it? Walk into school tomorrow morning and accuse Sienna of acting like a toddler?

"I'm just going to give the necklace back," said Lily. "And pretend like it never happened."

"No way!" said Reese. "That's letting her win. She booted you from a sleepover for not texting a boy. Who does that?"

"Um . . . Sienna?"

Reese rolled her eyes and threw a squishable in the shape of an avocado at Lily. It lightened the mood, which gave Lily the courage to ask, "What if . . . what if I never should have been invited to sleep over in the first place?"

"Why, Lil? Because you aren't cool enough to hang out with this girl?"

Yes, thought Lily. *Exactly*. But she didn't say anything out loud.

"Do you remember the great Hula Hoop disaster?"

asked Reese, lifting the avocado squishable from the floor and hugging it tight.

Lily nodded. When Reese was in eighth grade, two boys in her class made a "game" of trapping girls in Hula Hoops before the start of PE. They would drop the hoops around a girl's waist and shake her back and forth. One day the boys targeted Reese, rocking her so hard that she fell to the gym floor, bruising her hip bone. The teachers finally woke up to what had been going on when their mom threatened to initiate criminal charges against the boys unless they apologized in writing to every single girl who they'd targeted that year.

"Mom thought she'd handled it and that justice had been served," said Reese. "But something else happened that day that I've never told anyone."

Lily held still. There was so much of Reese's daily life that Lily did not know about—from the details of what she talked about with her friends at school, to the thoughts that drifted through her mind as she was falling asleep at night. So being the first to hear a long-held secret was like being handed a gift.

"What happened?" asked Lily quietly.

"Do you remember that girl Delia who moved away for high school?" said Reese. "She was pretty and popular . . . blah, blah, blah. Well, when I got up from the gym floor in tears, Delia walked up to me and said, 'I knew you wouldn't be cool enough to handle the attention.'"

"Why would she say that?"

"Because she was a Sienna. Even when I was so upset, she wanted me to know that I wasn't worthy." Reese shook her head and sighed. "Those boys were the worst. Their apology letters were pointless, and they were obviously not sorry at all. Every time I saw them for the rest of the year, I'd literally feel sick to my stomach. But Delia got inside me, you know?"

"You should have told someone," said Lily, even though she understood exactly why Reese had kept it private. After all, she was the one planning to slide Sienna's necklace through her locker slats rather than face her.

Reese shifted her position on Lily's bed, crossing her legs and sitting up. "The thing is, in my own way, I did start telling people. That summer I started ReesesPieces. It wasn't a revenge thing; that's not why I did it. But it did help me to get Delia's horrible voice out of my head. With every post that I put together I felt . . . cool, I guess. And in control. It's my feed and I get to say what I want, how I want. If someone trolls me in the comments, I just block them for life. And if Delia ever follows me . . ." Reese smiled and mimicked slitting her throat.

"Sienna follows you," said Lily. "She loves your style."

"Ooooh. Want me to block her when I get my phone back?"

"Yes!" said Lily. But as Reese gave her a double thumbs-up, Lily hesitated. "Wait. Will Sienna know?"

"It might take a while, but she'll probably figure it out when my posts stop appearing in her feed."

"Then don't," said Lily. "It's not worth it."

Reese sighed. "Up to you. But Lil, if you just give the necklace back and apologize, she'll keep going."

Lily nodded. But getting revenge by having Reese

block Sienna wasn't the answer. Neither was telling their mom. This was Lily's problem, and she would handle it her own way. If only she could figure out what her way was.

12. Will

Monday morning English class.

Because it was the start of a new week, Ms. Carter expected them to arrive chipper, focused, and ready to learn. Phones off. Eyes open.

It sounded brutal. But it wasn't that bad.

Also, Lily was in the class.

Will's fingers twitched at the memory of last night, staring at his phone, wondering if he should text her and then deciding not to.

As he walked into the classroom, Will realized that he'd made the right call. Lily's hand was cupped against her forehead, blocking her face as she doodled something in her notebook.

Will knew when someone was trying to disappear. He'd done it plenty of times himself.

Maybe Ms. Carter would notice and draw on her decades of teacherly wisdom to say the exact thing that Lily needed to hear? Will hoped so.

Except when Will turned to see the quote of the day that Ms. Carter always wrote on the smartboard, Mr. Stanlow was perched on the edge of the teacher desk instead.

"Ms. Carter called out sick," said Mr. Stanlow as Will took his seat. "I'm the best the school could do with such short notice. So here we are."

Theo and a few of his athlete friends cheered. Mr. Stanlow coached boys soccer and lacrosse. He had many loyal groupies.

"Now," continued Mr. Stanlow, "the incredibly wise Ms. Carter does not trust me to continue with the book you've been studying. So the theme of today's class is up to me. And no, we're not going to be spending class time debating the Eagles' choice of draft picks, pathetic as they may be." Mr. Stanlow ran his fingers through his hair. "What I would like us to discuss today is poetry."

As the groupies booed, Will checked on Lily. Her

hand was still blocking her face and she was biting her lower lip.

"Come on now, none of that. We can do this." Mr. Stanlow paused and winked. Will could have sworn that the wink was aimed in his exact direction. He lowered his eyes to his desk as Mr. Stanlow continued. "So, who wants to tell me what poetry is?"

When no one volunteered, Mr. Stanlow called on Theo.

"Um, I guess like romance and stuff," said Theo. "You know, that sometimes rhymes."

"Romance and stuff," repeated Mr. Stanlow. "That may or may not rhyme. Okay, we'll count that as a start. Who else can help me out?"

Sienna raised her hand. "Poetry is really, like, deep."

"Nice. I like that, Sienna. Who else?"

Will glanced at Lily. This was the point in the class where she would usually participate, coming up with a better answer than anyone before her.

Instead, there was silence. Total silence.

"Fine," said Mr. Stanlow. "If no one else is going

to help me out, I'll tell you what I think. I think poetry is about more than just romance. I think it's about life. All of it. The good, the bad, the ugly. It's your day put through a sieve so only the really important stuff is left." He paused. "Basically, it's life in all caps, no lowercase letters in sight."

Lowercase letters!

Did Mr. Stanlow really just say that? Will glanced at Lily.

Slowly, she looked up and smiled. Right. At. Him.

And his entire body warmed.

"So," continued Mr. Stanlow, "what we're going to do today is brainstorm some all caps life moments and use those as starting points for our own poetry. Don't worry. I'm not going to make you partner up and share. Poetry is an inside job. It's yours alone to undertake. I want you students to think about some everyday moments that have defined you and made who you are today. Then we're going to use those moments as inspiration for our own poems."

As they started on their lists, Mr. Stanlow went straight to Will's desk and crouched down.

"You know," he said, "this poetry assignment reminds me of another assignment. One handed out last week by yours truly. How's that one going?"

"It's going," said Will, relieved that it was actually the truth. In addition to the photo of Sienna and Cora walking away, he'd taken one that morning of a poster for the school dance. It was dangling by a taped corner, as if the poster was trying to escape the wall. Will shot the picture from the ground to emphasize the message.

Mr. Stanlow smiled. "So I can expect the photos for my empty bulletin board by the end of the week?"

"Yup," said Will.

"Great. I'm really looking forward to seeing what you come up with. Now write something deep or else Ms. Carter is going to come looking for me. And we both know who'd win that fight, right?"

"Her?" said Will.

Mr. Stanlow nodded. "No doubt."

Will laughed and Mr. Stanlow continued on toward the back of the room.

Before Will turned to his paper, he noticed Lily

stand and leave the classroom. It didn't seem like an emergency. But Lily was not the kind of student who normally exploited the bathroom excuse.

And Will wasn't the only one who noticed her leave. Sienna, who was sitting a row in front of Will, practically fell out of her seat.

"Did you lock your locker?" she whispered to Cora. "The thief is on the loose."

Cora laughed. "OMG, I hope so."

"What are you talking about?" asked Will.

"None of your business," snapped Cora.

"No, it's okay," said Sienna. "He deserves to know. I mean, it's kind of a matter of public safety."

There was a light, bouncy tone to Sienna's voice that made it clear something was brewing.

Will longed for his Power Putty. Although, he didn't trust himself not to chuck it at Sienna's face.

"Good point," agreed Cora. "Tell him."

"Lily stole my necklace," said Sienna. "Like, legit just took it."

"Her *evil-eye* necklace," added Cora, with joy. "We think Lily might be trying to curse Sienna."

Will shook his head. "You're joking, right?"

"Nope," said Sienna. "Not that I expect you to take my side or anything. I know how you feel about—"

"Shut up, Sienna," interrupted Will. "Just. Shut. Up."

While Will had shoved Sienna plenty of times when they were little, he hadn't touched her in years. But man, he really wanted to shake the smirk off her face.

First Stephanie on the phone to his dad. Now this.

Sienna was up to something.

And unlike his dad, Will didn't need to conduct a lengthy interview with some esteemed guest to know how the situation would end.

"Leave Lily alone, Sienna," he warned.

"Or what, *Will*?"

Will's brain pulsed. Throbbed. He was desperate for an answer that they both knew was out of reach.

"Or what, huh?" she repeated. "You're going to tell on me? Get me in trouble with my mom? She already hates me and worships you, so it wouldn't even be hard. You could just be your normal self and my mom would take your side against me, like always."

"Your mom doesn't hate you," said Cora. Her quiet voice broke through the quick, angry jabs of their exchange.

Will paused, thrown off-balance.

Sienna blinked rapidly, her telltale way of fighting back tears.

There was nothing left to do. To say.

When Cora reached out to touch Sienna, Sienna waved her off.

Will slid his elbow down his desk, pretending to refocus on the assignment, not all the rumors that Sienna might spread next.

13. Lily

Lily was grateful to discover that Mr. Stanlow was subbing for Ms. Carter. She'd tried to slip the envelope with the necklace inside into Sienna's locker before homeroom, but the hallways had been too crowded. A substitute teacher made faking an emergency trip to the bathroom during English way easier.

Even though the hallways were deserted, Lily's heart pounded as she dropped the envelope through the tilted slats of Sienna's locker. She pressed her ear to the metal, hoping to hear the sound of the chain settling against the bottom of the locker. Anything to confirm that the necklace was really and truly out of her life. Just as she was turning to go back to class, a different noise drifted into the hallway.

"Lily!" whispered a familiar voice.

It was Sasha. Lily was so surprised by her presence that she stumbled.

"OMG," said Sasha. "Did you just leave Sienna a secret note? Are you guys, like, best friends after just one sleepover?" Sasha leaned against a locker and pouted. "Because that's not fair, Lily. You're ours. She can't have you."

Lily stepped away from the locker. Away from the necklace. Away, she hoped, from anything that would make Sasha more suspicious. Sasha slid a piece of paper into her back pocket. When she crossed her arms, Lily noticed that Sasha's fingernails were painted in alternating maroon and blue. The colors of the elite soccer team.

"I'm just kidding," continued Sasha. "I know you'd never leave us for her. But what's with delivering a mysterious letter in the middle of class?"

Lily thought fast. "It's nothing. Just some font designs that I did for Sienna. Her name is really pretty in cursive, so I told her I'd come up with something special. You know I love S's."

"And you couldn't just hand it to her?" asked Sasha.

"It's more fun this way. You know, like a surprise."

Sasha laughed in agreement. Fun, joy, surprises—those were Sasha's favorite things. Thankfully, she loved them enough to believe Lily's lie. But before Lily could change the subject and ask why Sasha wasn't in her own class, Sasha's face shifted. "Seriously though, Lil," she said. "Are you and Sienna, like, besties now?"

Lily shook her head. "No. I mean, the sleepover was fun and everything. But we are definitely not besties."

"Oh, phew. Maddie said not to worry, but I couldn't stop thinking about the tragedy my life would be if you joined Sienna's friend group. I would never let her get away with stealing you."

It was a nice thing to say. The *right* thing to say. But it wasn't the truth. If Lily ditched Sasha and Maddie, they would still have their soccer tournaments with hotel sleepovers and, apparently, matching fingernails. It was Lily who would be left alone. The entire weekend had been proof of that. Which was why she needed to do all she could to put the disastrous sleepover behind her.

A distant door opened with a squeak, cutting through the silence. "We should probably get back," said Sasha.

"Yeah," agreed Lily. "What are you doing out here anyway?"

Sasha nodded at her own English class across the hall. "Oh, I saw you through the door and you never leave class. I just wanted to make sure you were okay."

Lily pulled Sasha into a quick hug. "Thanks, Sash. You're the greatest."

Sasha batted her eyelashes. "I know."

After English class, Lily watched as Sienna pulled the envelope from her locker, looked over her shoulder, and shoved it in her backpack. Lily even waved at Sienna—an embarrassing attempt to get Sienna to acknowledge the return of the necklace. But Sienna stormed off before Lily could make eye contact.

Then, all morning, the story of the stolen necklace trickled through the seventh grade. But it had never been stolen! And now it was returned! There was nothing scandalous to whisper about! Nonetheless, by lunch time it was clear: a gossip storm was heading Lily's way.

Instead of eating in their normal spot, Maddie and Sasha pulled Lily into the old bathrooms near the gym. No one ever used them unless they were desperate. Maddie checked the stalls while Sasha leaned against the entrance door, holding it shut.

"What is going on?" asked Maddie.

"You said the sleepover was fun," added Sasha.

"It was," said Lily in a chirpy voice that she halfway hoped her friends would realize was fake.

All morning she'd been ignoring stares and whispers, building a layer between her insides and what was happening outside. How much longer could she pretend that everything was fine?

"So why is Sienna saying that you stole her evil-eye necklace?" demanded Maddie. "She's telling everyone that you're trying to curse her. Like you're a witch or something."

"I don't know," said Lily. "I didn't steal anything."

"Come on, Lily," said Sasha. "It's us."

"Yeah," agreed Maddie. "We're your best friends."

Lily snapped. "I know it's you!" she yelled. "But *you* don't understand."

"We're just confused," said Sasha.

"It's not confusing! Sienna's lying. I accidentally took the necklace home because I was wearing it when I left Sienna's house, but then I gave it back." She looked at Sasha. "That's what I was doing in the hallway this morning. Putting it in her locker."

"But you said you were giving her some kind of name thingy. Why didn't you tell me the truth?"

The bathroom was so stuffy, with no windows or fresh air. Lily pushed up her sleeves to stop the sweat collecting on her skin. "It was too complicated."

"So, what?" said Maddie, her arms crossed. "Now we're too stupid to understand your life."

"No! That's not what I meant. It's just . . . there are some things that you don't understand. Like how it feels to be ditched and left behind all the time."

Sasha reached out for a hug. "But we'd never ditch you. You're *you*."

"Not on purpose," said Lily. "But ever since you made elites, it's always the two of you going off together to games and team dinners and stuff. I know you'd invite me if you could, but it doesn't change that I'm still always left behind."

"What are we supposed to do?" asked Maddie. "Quit soccer?"

"That's not what I mean."

"Then what *do* you mean, Lily?" continued Maddie. "Because we're here, trying to help our best friend in the whole entire world, and you're making it sound like everything is our fault."

When Sasha agreed with Maddie, nodding her head slowly, hesitantly, Lily understood that there was a new level of loneliness. One that was lower than hiding out in the library, or having an entire weekend with no plans, or skipping the middle school dance because you had no one to go with. It was the loneliness of the two people who you thought were your best friends listening to you, but not understanding.

Lily turned, went into a stall, and locked the door.

She wasn't sure how long Maddie and Sasha stayed in the bathroom, first gently asking to be let in, then banging on the door, then debating what to do next. It was hard to hear over her gulping sobs. And by the time she finally unlocked the stall and stepped out, they were both gone. Lunch was almost over and Lily was about to be late for math. She wiped her eyes with the bottom of her shirt and her nose with the scratchy school toilet paper, stuffing an extra clump into her pocket, just to be safe. With her gaze down and her shoulders hunched, Lily walked to her locker to switch her binders.

She almost made it into the safety of the math classroom, where Mr. Myron would probably notice that something was wrong, but not make a big deal of it. He was cool that way. But instead of sliding into her assigned seat, Lily was met outside the classroom door by Sienna, with Cora at her side. Lily pressed her binder to her chest like a shield. The gesture prevented her hands from shaking, but it did nothing to stop the trembling sensation in her chin. Her eyes had barely dried. A new round of tears were right there, brewing, begging to be released.

"So, Lily," said Sienna. "Are you ready to give it back yet? You know, the necklace you *stole*."

"I didn't steal it. You gave it to me, remember? I just forgot to take it off."

Sienna gave Cora an I-told-you-so glance. "I so did *not* give it to you."

"You know what I mean," said Lily, pleading with her eyes for Sienna to acknowledge the truth.

"Whatever," said Sienna. "But why do you still have it?"

"I don't. I put it in your locker. It's in an envelope with your name on it. I swear. I saw you . . ."

"In my locker?" interrupted Sienna. A flash crossed her face, almost as if a ghostly reflection of an envelope was floating before her eyes. But just as quickly as the expression arrived, Sienna shook it off. "You know what, Lily, who cares about the necklace. You're annoying. That's exactly what you are. *Annoying*."

The way the term left Sienna's mouth was so final, so authoritative, as if she was speaking on behalf of every single person that they both knew, that it pierced Lily's heart.

And she could not help but think, *Maybe you're right*.

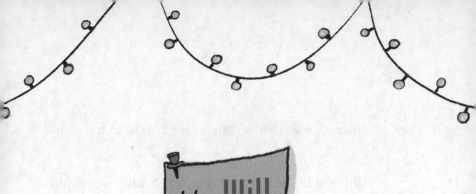

14. Will

"What do we want for dinner?" asked Will's dad on Monday evening. "Something well-balanced and nutritious? Or . . ."

"Shake Shack?" said Will.

"Exactly what I was thinking."

Over burgers, fries, and milkshakes, they talked about climbing and the Eagles' chances of making the playoffs. When his dad began to chant the Eagles fight song—"Fly, Eagles Fly"—Will threw a crinkled fry at his forehead.

As the fry dropped to the table, his dad's eyes narrowed. Will braced himself for a lecture. Maybe something about finding the pause before giving into impulses. Or how actions that might seem harmless affect others. The possibilities were endless.

Instead, his dad laughed. He threw a fry right back.

Will's shoulders dropped in relief. This was going to be a good dinner. They would eat, laugh, and kinda sorta talk.

He took a long sip of his vanilla milkshake as he settled back into the booth.

"So," said his dad. "Hit me."

"Just did," joked Will, crunching a french fry.

"You know what I mean. Give me an update. What are the chances you reconsidered going to the school dance this weekend?"

"Zero."

"Go with Gavin, at least. Could be fun."

"To go to a dance with Gavin? You're joking."

His dad tilted his head and smiled. At first Will assumed his dad was acknowledging the stupidity of his own suggestion. But then he said, "You know who loved to dance?"

Will looked down at the ketchup pooled on his tray. The switch in his dad's tone of voice gave the answer away. "Mom?"

"Yep," said his dad, nodding. "Loved it. Before our wedding she made me take ballroom dance lessons with this short old guy who had a studio attached to his house. I was so terrible at learning the steps that the instructor and I would spend most of the lesson dancing together while your mom looked on and laughed. The guy had this firm, round belly that I would bump into when I was supposed to spin him. It was horrible. And humiliating. But also totally worth it because it cracked your mom up. God, I loved her laugh." He shook his head and sighed.

"I wish I could have seen that," said Will.

"I wish *I'd* gotten it on camera. Although, then it might have gone viral in the worst possible way."

His dad gathered the stray napkins and straw wrappers from their table and stood up. When Will remained seated, distracted with a sudden realization, his dad paused. "Are you coming?"

"I was just . . . Do you think Mom would have posted a video like that? You know, something so embarrassing."

"Actually," said his dad, placing his tray back down

on the table. "Now that I think about it, probably not."

It was like gripping the lowest hold on the climbing wall. A start.

Will wanted to keep going and suggest that his dad stop sharing so much as well. But the restaurant was loud and crowded. Two teenagers were lurking by their table, a food buzzer in each of their hands, hoping to claim their seats.

They made their way to the exit. "Mind if I stop on the way home to pick up a prescription?" asked his dad when they stepped outside.

Will shook his head. "No problem." Was his dad changing the subject on purpose? Or did he think their conversation was over? It was impossible to tell.

They walked toward the pharmacy in silence. Will waited outside, frustration at his dad's obliviousness growing with each passing minute. He wandered down the block.

There was a florist and a stationery store. Both were closed.

The next shop sold jewelry and its lights were still on. In the window display, hanging from a branch, was a collection of evil-eye necklaces.

Just like the one Sienna sometimes wore. That she claimed Lily had stolen.

The stirring inside Will's chest that came from talking about his mom was replaced by something prickly. The drama of the day came rushing back.

Sienna had probably lost the necklace and was blaming someone else for her mistake. She'd find it in a day. On the floor behind her desk. Or between the pillows of her bed.

Maybe Lily had just done something innocent like admire the necklace. Sienna did have good style. He had to admit that she was a trendsetter.

Suddenly Will's heart began to race. His hands grew clammy.

Should he just go in and look at the necklaces?

Looking was harmless. It didn't mean he was looking on behalf of anyone in particular.

Will checked the sidewalk to make sure that his dad hadn't come out of the pharmacy. Then he stepped inside.

The store was packed with so many delicate,

sparkling pieces that Will stuffed his hands in his pockets. As he approached the necklace display, a saleswoman came up to him. "Need any help?"

Will shook his head. "No, thanks."

"I can barely keep these in stock," she said, ignoring his response and walking toward the window. "I just got a few in today and they won't last long. Would you like to see one?" Without waiting for an answer, she slid a necklace from the branch and placed it in her palm. "Do you know about evil eyes?"

"Kind of."

"Good. So you know that they protect the wearer from curses and unkind words."

"Yeah," said Will. "Right."

Will did not actually believe that the necklaces held any kind of power, but he wished they did. Lily could probably use something like that.

"I can wrap it up for you if you'd like," said the saleswoman. "Put it in a nice box?"

At Philly Rocks, Dustin coached his climbers to choose the path of least resistance. The least strenuous way to the top. The message echoed in his mind.

Why fight the pushy saleswoman? The path of least resistance pointed toward making the purchase and leaving the store before his dad called his phone, wondering where he was.

"Okay," said Will. "I'll get that one."

Will followed her to the counter, opening the app on his phone to check his Greenlight account. He had weeks of allowance saved. More than enough to cover the fifteen-dollar price.

As he stood at the counter and paid, waiting while the saleswoman placed the necklace in a small white box, Will stood a little taller.

He slid the box into his pocket as he fled the store, grateful that his dad was halfway down the block, facing the opposite direction.

This was private. And Will was determined to keep it that way.

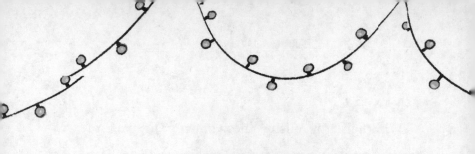

15. Lily

All day long Sienna's voice echoed in Lily's head. *You're annoying. That's exactly what you are. Annoying.* Lily was stuck inside a maze with no idea how to get out. She could imagine how other people would handle the situation. Reese would channel her hurt into some beautiful fashion post. Maddie and Sasha would run for as long as it took to find the exit. Will would climb out, no matter how high the wall. But what was she supposed to do?

Maddie and Sasha weren't hopelessly mad at her. If she texted the group chat with an apology, they would totally respond. But then she would have to open up about what had really happened at the sleepover, and it was all too fresh, too painful. As Lily uncapped a new marker and began to doodle on a piece of notebook paper, she found herself writing a new name—Will.

She experimented with the bottom arcs of the *w* and the slants of the double *l*. The longer she drew, the more tempted she was to text him. Will would lighten her mood somehow. Maybe he would even make her laugh. But first she had to figure out what to write.

Lily remembered that Will's dad hosted a podcast called *Dr. Dad*. Apparently he talked about Will a lot on the show. Maybe listening to *Dr. Dad* would help her get to know Will a little better without actually having to speak to him? Lily searched her phone, unsuccessfully trying to find the podcast app. Her mom must have deleted it when she was setting up Lily's phone, and she wasn't allowed to download anything new without triggering the parental permission function. If she did that, then her parents would want to know why she had a sudden interest in podcasts, which ones she wanted to listen to, and for what reason. *Ugh.* Reese had taught her about cross-branding and how Instagram influencers sometimes started podcasts and vice versa. Maybe the *Dr. Dad* podcast also had an Instagram account?

Lily typed "Dr. Dad" into the search bar. A picture of young Will sitting in his dad's lap came up. She opened the feed, ready to scroll as fast as she could to maximize her screen time since she only had a minute or so left for the day. But Lily didn't make it past the very first post, which was a photo of Will looking at a display of necklaces. The images were a little blurry, as if taken from outside a window, but the details flashed into her brain—boom, boom, boom.

The necklaces had evil-eye pendants with turquoise center stones and silver chains.

Will was studying them, his hands in his pockets.

They were just like Sienna's necklace. The one Sienna told everyone that Lily had stolen.

Her hands shaking, Lily read the caption:

Top-secret breaking news: I think someone has his first crush. The little man ditched me tonight after dinner and look where I found him! At a jewelry store, possibly buying something special for someone special? I'll be honest, this was one of those moments when I really missed his mom. She would have known exactly what to do while my first instinct was to storm the place. But I waited outside, trying to be the cool dad and give the little man some space. Don't know who this purchase is for, but I know she's a lucky girl. Any advice on middle school romance would be greatly appreciated. I need my parenting tribe right now! Please comment below.

Before Lily could read the comments, her phone locked. She was left with a time limit expiration and a twisting pain in her stomach. Will had heard the stolen necklace rumor and he'd bought Sienna a replacement. Sienna was Will's "someone special."

Suddenly the whole situation made complete sense. No wonder Sienna had been so insistent about Lily texting Will and setting them up for the dance. Will had a crush on Sienna. A crush so big, probably building for so long, that he bought Sienna gifts even though she had no interest in him. Sienna was using her, trying to get Will off her case by presenting Lily as a distraction. But what about Will? As painful as it was to admit, Lily now understood that he had done nothing other than be nice enough to return her water bottle and play along with an inside joke. The importance of their relationship, the moments when she was certain Will was looking at her, thinking of her, were all in Lily's head.

She was an annoying, romantic reject. This was so much bigger than just Sienna being mean. It was Sienna liking Jake, and Will liking Sienna. It was Maddie liking Bex, and Sasha not knowing. It was Maddie and Sasha spending all their time playing soccer and then ganging up on her in the bathroom. It was her mom in an endless fight with Reese. It was her dad acting like he was helpless against the constant conflict. It was the stupidity of her crush on Will, which she couldn't even decide was an official crush and hadn't told her best (ex-best?) friends about. It was everything!

You need to find a way to stop her. That's what Reese had said. But how could Lily stop all of *them*? All of *it*? She couldn't. But maybe she could start by trying to make things better with Maddie and Sasha. She needed them, even when it felt like they didn't need her. Lily could not face school tomorrow all alone.

She checked the time. 8:56 p.m. Their phones all locked for the night at nine p.m. Lily texted the group chat:

> Hi
> U guys there?

Seconds later Sasha responded with a screenful of smiley face emojis. Maddie did the same with alternating heart and unicorn emojis. Lily smiled at the colorful stream. When it eventually slowed, Maddie said they should switch to FaceTime, texting:

> If it's ok with Lily

They connected, each in their own beds with Sasha hanging upside down. After a beat of awkward silence, Maddie spoke. "Sorry about today, Lily."

"Please don't be mad at us," added Sasha. "Pretty, pretty, pretty please."

"I'm not mad," said Lily. "I'm more embarrassed. Everyone at school's talking about me, but they only know Sienna's side. It felt like you were doing the same."

"So tell people the truth," said Maddie.

If they had been in person, Lily would have subtly elbowed Maddie who, as best Lily could tell, was still hiding her own secret from Sasha. Over FaceTime, that was impossible. So instead Lily said, "I don't know how. Sienna's never going to admit that I returned the necklace. And it's not like I can just walk down the hall shouting to everyone that she's a liar."

Lily paused. She almost explained that Will having a crush on Sienna made the situation even more complicated. But that would have to wait. It was 8:58. They only had two more minutes to talk.

"I have an idea," said Sasha as she did a back somersault off her bed and walked across her room. "Let's make a giant sign that says 'Sienna is a liar.' We can tape it to the DJ stand so everyone at the dance sees it."

"Sash," said Maddie, softly. "We're not going to the dance, remember?" Even over FaceTime, Lily could see the sympathy in Maddie's face.

"Exactly!" said Sasha. "That's why this plan is perfect. No one will know that it's us!" Sasha put her phone down on her desk, leaving Maddie and Lily with a view of her white ceiling. A few seconds later, she focused the phone on a piece of paper. "Here, this is what it will look like."

Lily laughed. Sasha had written the letters in red marker with a large brown poop emoji at the end. She was clearly joking, trying to make them laugh in her Sasha way.

"Nice *s*," said Lily, actually impressed. It was way better than Sasha's normal sloppy handwriting.

"Thanks!" said Sasha. "I've actually been practicing. You know, in your honor, Lily."

"It's true," said Maddie. "Coach likes us to take notes on plays. But Sasha's always doodling letters instead."

"That's because I'm always benched during games. What's the point of—"

The clock turned to nine p.m. and their screens locked. Lily held her phone for another moment, as if to stay in the company of her friends. There was so much more to say and figure out, but at least they were talking. The harder stuff—like how she was supposed to handle liking Will *and* talking to him *and* knowing that he secretly liked Sienna—would have to wait until tomorrow.

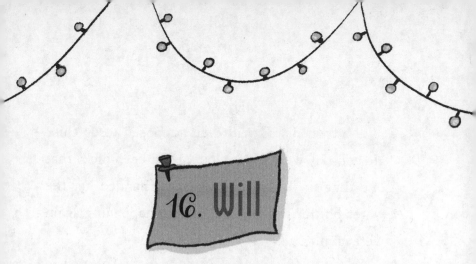

16. Will

Someday Will would climb Everest. Cotopaxi. The Alps.

He would trek over ice glaciers and carry weeks of supplies on his back.

But somehow, this little white box with the necklace inside seemed impossibly heavy.

He'd placed it in his backpack on Tuesday morning, and it had remained there all day. Now it was Wednesday, and the necklace was still in the deep dark pit of his backpack.

What was he supposed to do? Walk up to Lily and hand the necklace to her?

Would she understand that the gesture was meant to fix things? Or would she think it was random and creepy?

And when was Will even supposed to do this? He and Lily were never alone. He'd been lucky that one time in the hallway when he handed her the water bottle. The chances of that happening again were slim.

But fate was, for once, in his favor. When they were shuffling out of English class, Lily ended up right in front of him with no one else close by.

Ms. Carter was back, but Mr. Stanlow's definition of poetry was fresh in Will's mind. Being so close to Lily with the necklace hidden in his backpack was definitely a capital *L* Life moment.

Will cleared his throat. "At least we didn't have to do poetry today."

"Yeah," said Lily.

"Like, what would we even write about?"

"No idea," she answered.

Lily was being more clipped than normal. But Will kept trying. "The Lowercase Letters suck at lyrics," he said. "All our songs are gonna be just humming."

Will began to hum. When Lily didn't react, he added, "We'll have to hire one of those little kids who never shut up to write our music. Remember? The preschool kids with the maracas?"

"I remember," said Lily, finally smiling.

Will really liked to make her smile.

"And the leather jackets," he continued. "We should work on finding those."

"Right," said Lily. "And maybe some shredded jeans. Leather boots."

"With metal studs."

"Totally!"

As Lily laughed, Will's heart floated into his throat.

But suddenly her expression changed. She brought her finger to her lips.

"You okay?" asked Will.

"Yeah," said Lily defensively. "Why wouldn't I be?"

Before Will could answer, Lily mumbled something about needing to go and waved goodbye. Without even a "see ya later," she walked into the hallway.

It was a diss, plain and simple.

Will's stomach hurt. Like there was a jumble of loose dirt churning inside.

He glanced at the hallway clock. Morning recess was fifteen minutes long. He didn't want to grab food with Gavin or chill in the hallway. It had just started to rain, so he couldn't go to the courtyard. But it was impossible to stay still with this ache inside. He needed a distraction.

His "How I See It" photos were due by the end of the day on Friday. Two days from now.

Just that morning, Will had taken a picture of Theo and Jake kicking a soccer ball on the front lawn. He caught the ball at the midpoint of its arc, sailing through the air. Will hadn't intended to get Theo and Jake in the image, but he actually liked the way the picture turned out.

It was as if they were all little again and playing at recess.

At least, that's how Mr. Stanlow would see it. And Will, his stomach still in knots, wanted to show the opposite side of seventh grade.

With the camera in his backpack, Will walked toward the trash room.

The Environmental Club had recently started a

food composting project. He envisioned snapping a photograph of heaps of wet, moldy food.

But when he pulled on the latch that opened the door to the outside bin, it was locked.

Same for the door that led to the dumpsters.

The only trash Will could access were the recycling bins, which were neatly organized by material. Someone had clearly gotten in trouble and been assigned Will's former punishment. And Will had to admit—they'd done a good job. Better than he ever had.

Will turned one of the blue bins over to use as a step stool.

He took a photo of crumpled aluminum cans. Secretly, they represented his crushed soul.

He took another of his foot raised against the dirty wall, with the rim of the recycling bin in the corner. It came out great. Like he was trying to kick through the plaster.

The falling poster. Sienna's and Cora's backs. The soccer ball. Plus, the two he'd just taken. He still had five pictures to go.

Will turned and assessed the bin of paper

recycling. It had artistic potential. There was blank and lined paper. Some with typed words and others with handwritten notes. Lots of math worksheets. A few long essays.

And there, on the top, was a white envelope with Sienna's name printed in pretty looping handwriting.

Next to the name was a flower.

Just like the one Lily always drew beside her own name.

Maybe Sienna had copied Lily's signature flower? Or maybe Lily had drawn it for Sienna before everything exploded?

Either way, the crisp white envelope amid the pile of dirty crumpled paper captured his attention. He aimed the camera at the envelope and took a close-up picture.

But as soon as it printed, Will's brain returned to his body.

He couldn't turn this one in as a reflection of how he saw school.

There were too many ways to interpret a clean envelope with Sienna's name and a flower. One was that Sienna belonged in a pile of garbage. But because Sienna was so popular, it could also be played the opposite way. As some kind of statement that Sienna was somehow better and more special than everything around her.

No matter what, the photo would draw attention to someone who already got loads of it. Someone who was making trouble for Lily.

Garbage smelled, but turning in this image stunk of betrayal.

Will slid the picture into his back left pocket, separate from the rest of the photos, which were tucked into his right pocket.

As he left the recycling room with the separated images, a tingle of guilt nagged at him. Should he be worried about the other pictures? After all, Sienna and Cora hadn't known that Will was taking the photo. They hadn't agreed. Neither had Jake or Theo. And now their pictures were going to be displayed for everyone to see.

Maybe they didn't want to be put in the spotlight. Maybe it would be embarrassing for them in the way it was embarrassing for Will to be spoken about on *Dr. Dad*.

His dad had agreed that his mom wouldn't have shared their dance rehearsal video. Why was Will sharing these photos? And why was he being asked to do it by a guidance counselor?

Wasn't it Mr. Stanlow's job to know this stuff? He was there to *guide*.

Yes, he could give a good lecture. But maybe he didn't always know what he was talking about. Time to find out.

Mr. Stanlow was at his desk when Will knocked on the door. He looked up with such excitement that Will almost turned around.

"Just the man I was hoping to see," said Mr. Stanlow. "You got anything for me?"

Will pulled out the stack of photos from his right pocket. "Kind of."

Mr. Stanlow rocked his head as if moving to the beat of music. "I'll take 'kind of.' It beats the alternative. Let me see what you've got."

Mr. Stanlow began to flip through the photos.

First came the photo of Sienna and Cora walking away. Then the picture of the dangling dance poster. Mr. Stanlow placed those side by side on his desk. He held the photo of Theo and Jake at arm's distance and put it down beside the other two. Next came the ones that Will had taken in the recycling room.

"Decent," said Mr. Stanlow. "But I was hoping for some more people in these photos."

Will shifted his gaze to the row of My Little Pony figurines. "That's part of the problem," he said.

Mr. Stanlow leaned forward and clasped his hands on his desk. "Will, buddy. You're a great kid. There are a lot of people at this school who would love to be your friend."

"But it's up to them," said Will quietly.

"I'm not following," said Mr. Stanlow.

Will reached over to the windowsill and grabbed an orange My Little Pony with a yellow mane and tail—Applejack, maybe? He'd left his Power Putty at home and just needed something to do with his hands. "What I mean is," he said as he twisted the pony's tail, "you shouldn't force kids to be friends with someone against their will. And you shouldn't put their pictures on some stupid bulletin board without their permission."

Mr. Stanlow leaned back, as if replaying Will's words in his mind. "I think I understand," he said.

Will stopped spinning the pony's tail. *Did he?*

"And you know," continued Mr. Stanlow, "that's my bad. I didn't think about the assignment from every perspective. What if, for example, there's a student who doesn't want their picture posted on a bulletin board for everyone to see."

"And analyze," said Will, practically cutting Mr. Stanlow off. "And, like, evaluate. For whether they look cool or stupid or whatever."

"Yes," said Mr. Stanlow, nodding. "Because that's bound to happen. I get that now. And I didn't before."

"Okay," said Will, standing. "That's all I wanted to tell you."

"You sure, Will? Nothing else you want to talk about? Because this was really helpful."

"Nah," said Will. "That's it."

Will was almost out the door when Mr. Stanlow

called, "You taking my Applejack? Do I at least get a moment to say goodbye?"

Will shook his head and laughed. He was still holding the figurine. He tossed the pony back to Mr. Stanlow, who caught it with one hand.

"Nice toss," said Mr. Stanlow.

"Nice catch," said Will.

"Teamwork," said Mr. Stanlow. "It's important."

Will didn't respond, but he couldn't deny that he agreed.

17. Lily

By lunchtime, with the rain still coming down, Lily gave up all hope of eating outdoors, where she and Maddie and Sasha could actually speak privately. They managed to get seats next to one another in the cafeteria, but their table was crowded with other kids. Instead of talking about Will, or even the necklace rumors that were still going around, they talked about Jake burping paint can lids in art and the geniuses in Sasha's advanced math class.

Their fight was still fresh enough that talking at all was a relief, but it didn't help Lily figure anything out. Maddie's dad was driving to soccer practice and, unlike Sasha's mom, he was always early. So at dismissal, when the rain finally cleared, Lily headed straight home. She was one block from school when she sensed someone walking behind her. *Please not Sienna,* she thought as she glanced over her shoulder.

It was Will, just a few steps behind. He waved, then immediately dropped his hand to his side. Lily waved back and kept moving, but she was acutely aware of her backpack and the sway of her pom-pom key chains; the hem of her jacket and how it suddenly seemed to be bunching up around her waist. With Will behind her, every detail mattered in a whole new way. When Lily stopped at the light and Will caught up, she was actually relieved. It was better to see him next to her than picture him behind her.

They crossed the street side by side. Lily expected him to make a joke, but Will was quiet. As the seconds passed, Lily had a harder and harder time deciding what to do. Should she keep walking in silence? Or start a conversation? He was so close, walking at the exact same pace. So why was he silent?

"What?" she finally demanded.

"Nothing," said Will.

"Then why are you . . . ?" She brought her hands together to indicate the distance between them.

"It's a sidewalk."

"Fine, but you don't have to be all quiet and weird. I know . . ." Lily paused. Should she just come out and say it? She'd wanted so badly to tell Maddie and Sasha first. But that hadn't been possible, and the urge was still burning inside her. She took a quick inhale and said, "I know you like Sienna."

Will recoiled. "I like *Sienna*?"

Lily nodded.

"You're kidding."

"It's okay, Will. I'm not offended. Everyone always likes her."

"Lily." He reached out and touched her arm. It was only a second, but they both looked at the spot where his fingers had met her sleeve.

If they were going to be friends, or at least not awkward classmates, there was something Lily needed him to understand. "Just for the record," she said, "I gave Sienna's necklace back to her. I put it in her locker."

"Did you tell her that?"

"Of course! I told her that I put the necklace in an

envelope inside her locker. I even saw her take it out. It doesn't matter, though, because no one believes me. I'm sure you heard the rumors that I stole the necklace to put a curse on her. As if anything I did would ever affect Sienna." Lily paused. "It's like she's rubber and I'm glue. Or whatever that babyish rhyme is."

"The Lowercase Letters would know."

Lily was about to say that she wasn't in the mood for jokes, but then Will pretended to shake imaginary maracas, turning circles in a silly dance as they continued down the sidewalk. It was embarrassing. And also the funniest thing Lily had ever seen. She laughed and laughed. Her entire body rocked as she begged Will to stop dancing. It was simply too funny.

"Seriously, Will," she said as she struggled to catch her breath. "I know you believe her, too. I saw the necklace that you bought."

Will froze. "What are you talking about?"

"The necklace from the jewelry store," explained Lily. "Your dad posted about it on Instagram."

Will's face changed from confusion to understanding to anger. "On Instagram?" he asked. "Can I see?"

"Don't you have an account?" asked Lily.

"I'm not allowed. Are you?"

"I only have five minutes during school days." Lily opened the app and quickly searched *Dr. Dad*. When the post came up, she handed the phone to Will. His hand began to tremble as he read.

"I didn't know he took this. Or posted it."

Lily looked at the picture. Seeing it through Will's eyes, she noticed new details, like the reflection of his dad on the glass storefront and the twisted angle of Will's shoulders. He definitely did not know that the photo was being taken. Lily's parents weren't on social media, but if they ever shared a similar picture of her publicly, she would be annoyed as well. Lily thought about all the care that Reese took to ensure that Lily looked her absolute coolest before posting pictures of her on ReesesPieces. Poor Will.

"I'm sure it won't matter to Sienna," she said.

"She'll just be flattered that you bought her a necklace."

Will shook his head. He looked straight into her eyes. "Lily, I didn't buy the necklace for Sienna. I bought it for you."

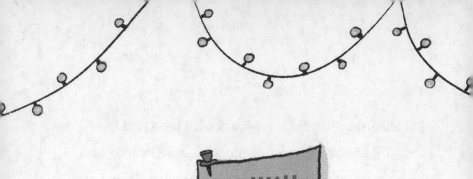

18. Will

They stood in a thick silence.

Will wanted to summon the familiar anger—how could his dad take a secret photo? How could he think it was okay to embarrass Will like that? For what, likes from strangers?

But the primary emotion pulsing through Will's body was endless, bottomless hurt.

And to top it off, Will had blurted out the truth about the necklace to Lily. That was its own kind of embarrassing pain.

Now he had to brace himself for the possibility of rejection, which would be coming any second.

Instead, Lily shifted her backpack on her shoulders. She nodded toward an empty bench on the sidewalk and asked, "Do you want to sit?"

Will sank onto the wood slats. He dropped his head between his legs.

Lily sat next to him. In her stillness, Will sensed that she understood at least some of the thoughts rushing through his brain.

Then she whispered, "Thank you."

He looked up. And gave her a tight smile.

"For buying me a necklace," continued Lily. "No one's ever bought me anything before. I mean, not someone like you. Can I see it?"

Will reached into his backpack and pulled out the box. He handed it to her.

All those hours that he'd carried the necklace around, he had never been able to imagine how he would present it to her. Certainly not like this.

Lily lifted the lid. The necklace chain was tangled from being tossed around inside his backpack. Carefully, she untangled it and clasped the chain around her neck.

The necklace looked great on her.

"I love it," she said.

Will smiled.

"Except, I can't wear it to school. People might think it's Sienna's and . . ." Her voice trailed off.

"Right," said Will. "Of course." He hadn't thought about that, but it made sense.

Lily kicked at a fallen acorn. "I just wish I could prove it."

The necklace. Lily's sigh of defeat. His dad's picture. They made him remember something. "You said you put an envelope inside Sienna's locker, right?" he asked.

Lily nodded.

"With her name on it?"

"Yeah. On the front."

Will pulled the Polaroid picture, the one that he'd held back to keep private, from his back pocket.

Lily gasped and grabbed the photo from his fingers. "That's it! That's the envelope! It's my handwriting and my signature flower. Where—"

"It was in the recycling room at school. I was doing this assignment for Mr. Stanlow and . . ." He paused. "Long story. But I took this today at recess."

Lily slid her fingers across the image, as if she was

trying to enlarge it. "I wish we could zoom in. The envelope looks like it's still sealed. Doesn't it?"

Will leaned over. Their foreheads almost touched. "Yeah. I mean, the envelope's definitely not torn at the top. Maybe it's ripped on the back, but I don't think so. It looks too crisp."

"So Sienna threw it out without even opening it?" asked Lily.

Will shrugged. "Maybe she gets so much fan mail in her locker that she can't keep up." It was a joke, obviously. Except Lily didn't laugh.

"It doesn't make sense," she said. "If someone left an envelope in my locker, I'd definitely open it. I'd be way too curious to just toss it in the recycling. Maybe she threw it out by accident? We have to ask."

Will leaned back against the bench, hesitating.

"Come on," said Lily, bumping her shoulder against his. "What would the Lowercase Letters do?"

"Cry? And then go home to take a nap?"

"Nice try. We're figuring this out." Lily already had her phone in her hand, except then she froze. "What do I say?"

"Something short and sweet," said Will. "Like, 'What the hell!'"

"If I text that, Sienna will ghost me. Or twist it somehow so I look like an idiot. I think we have to find her and ask in person."

"Do we really?" Will sighed, but it was a fake sigh. Lily's energy was contagious.

Will stood up, tightened the straps of his backpack, and reached out his hand to pull her up, too. "All right," he said. "Let's do this."

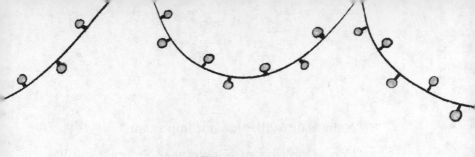

19. Lily

Will walked up to the doorman of Sienna's building and gave him a high five.

"Yo, Frogman," said the doorman. "Where you been?"

"Around," said Will. Then he smiled. "Just not around here. Can we go up?"

The doorman nodded and motioned them through. "I'll call to let them know that the legendary Frogman is on his way." He lifted the receiver of the intercom system. "Wait. Who are you here to see? The queen or the princess?"

Will blushed. "The princess," he mumbled, as if he didn't want Lily to hear.

"Tough break, Frogman. Don't think she's home from school yet. Want to leave her a message?"

"Nah," said Will. "It's not important."

"Cool. Don't be such a stranger, Frogman. I miss you."

Lily stayed silent through the exchange, mostly grateful that the doorman was not the same one who'd been on duty during the horrible sleepover.

"Let me guess," she said, nodding back toward the front door. "You're Frogman and Sienna is . . . Princess? Sienna said your families were close, but I didn't realize that meant code names."

"I spent a ton of time at Sienna's when I was younger," said Will. He paused. "Our moms were best friends."

The mention of Will's mom sent chills up Lily's arms. "I'm really sorry about your mom," she said. "I remember when it happened."

Will nodded. "Yeah. Thanks."

They took a few more steps in silence, then Lily glanced at him and asked, "What's up with Frogman?"

Will smiled. "I guess when I was little, like majorly little, I used to crouch down by the elevator and jump for the buttons. Like a frog. He never lets me forget it."

"Don't tell me you said *ribbit* as you jumped."

Will crouched down with a mischievous smile. Lily pretended to cover her eyes as he exploded from the sidewalk in a leap, complete with frog sound effects. When Lily finally stopped laughing, Will asked, "So . . . Sienna?"

Oh, right.

"Where do you think she is?" continued Will.

"I have an idea," said Lily. "This way."

Sienna was indeed sitting at a side table in the Secret Coffee Shop, scrolling through her phone while she sipped a drink. Drips of chocolate syrup ran down the sides of the clear glass cup. Even sitting all alone, Sienna looked so confident. More like one of Reese's high school friends than a middle schooler. Lily was furious about the false rumors that Sienna had been spreading, but she still felt a pinch of jealousy.

"Bingo," whispered Will.

Lily led the way through the maze of chairs to Sienna's table.

When Lily tapped her on the shoulder, Sienna looked up from her screen and blinked. "Ah, the lovebirds. Look at you two. You're so cute together." She put her phone down and brought her hands to her chest. "And just in time for the dance on Friday."

"Shove it, Sienna," said Will.

"Don't be embarrassed. I told you to trust me, Will. I know soulmates when I see them."

"You don't know anything."

"I know a lot more than you," Sienna shot back.

They were fighting the way she and Reese sometimes fought, Lily realized. Like siblings, which meant they could go on forever. So Lily held out her hand and asked Will for the picture. She placed it in the center of the round table.

The sharpness in Sienna's face—her focused eyes, her firmly set lips—disappeared. Her mouth opened in surprise and she slid to the back of her metal seat, as if trying to get distance from the picture. Then Sienna shook her head and said, "What? It's an envelope with my name on it. Who cares."

"It's the envelope that I left in your locker with the necklace inside," said Lily. "You threw it away without even opening it."

"You know she's telling the truth, Sienna," said Will. "I can see it in your face."

Lily agreed. Sienna's guilt was obvious. But there was something else in her eyes—tears. A slow build of shiny, glistening wetness. Sienna was using every ounce of control to hold them back, but she was losing the battle. Lily sat down in an empty seat. She motioned for Will to do the same.

"What is it?" asked Lily.

Sienna wiped her cheeks. "So I threw out a stupid letter! Kill me! Or better yet, report me to Mr. Myron. Maybe he can strangle me with a pair of his ugly disgusting socks."

Lily caught Will's eye, confused. What did Mr. Myron, who taught seventh-grade math and had terrible taste in socks, have to do with this?

"Sienna," said Lily. "What are you talking about?"

Sienna shook her head and wrapped her lips tight around her straw, a single tear leaking from her left eye as she drank. "Nothing," she mumbled. When Lily and Will both gave her disbelieving looks, she finally glanced up. "Ugh. Fine. Whatever. If you have to know, I thought the letter was from someone else. I thought it was . . . from Sasha."

"Sasha?" asked Lily. "My Sasha?"

"*Your* Sasha? What, now you own her?"

"That's not what I'm saying. Just . . . why would Sasha write you a letter?"

Sienna wiped her cheeks against her sleeve as more tears fell. "I suck at math, okay. So sometimes Sasha gives me the homework answers. It's not like cheating on an actual test or anything. It's not like a *crime*. It's the same thing as a tutor but way cheaper, and my mom doesn't have to know."

Lily shook her head. "Sasha wouldn't do that."

Sienna attempted a snobby laugh, but the tears made it sound more like a snort. "She would and she did. Five bucks for each homework assignment. She slips them in my locker and then I slip the money into hers. It worked perfectly until I basically failed the last homework assignment and I realized that she'd messed me up on purpose. Like, thanks a lot, Sasha. What did I ever do to you? Anyway, so when I saw the letter I threw it in the recycling without opening it. I swear. I didn't know the necklace was inside."

Lily's first instinct was to keep defending her friend. Sasha wouldn't cheat! She wouldn't give Sienna homework answers for money! No way! Except, the pieces of Sienna's story fit. Lily thought back to running into Sasha at Sienna's locker during class. Maybe Sasha hadn't just seen Lily walking past? Maybe she'd been there to deliver her own envelope to Sienna? And there were the random comments, like Sasha saying that she'd been practicing her *s*'s so they looked like Lily's, and her mom starting a side business to help cover Sasha's soccer expenses. It all made a sad kind of sense. But there was something else Lily still couldn't understand.

"Why did you act like you wanted to be friends with me?" she asked.

"Because I actually *did* want to!" said Sienna. "Is that a crime? I saw that picture your sister posted on her Instagram and I thought you looked, I don't know, cool. Then I found out that Will had a crush on you and I was like—win-win. Maybe we'd become friends and you and Will could go to the dance together. But then you were such a scaredy-cat at the sleepover and I just snapped."

Sienna paused to wipe her nose. "All I do is try," she continued. "I try to do well in math, but I suck at it. I try to set people up for the dance so they can be happy when, FYI, I don't even have a date myself. But no one ever says, like, 'Thanks, Sienna.' Or 'You're so kind, Sienna.' They just think I'm bossy and controlling. And probably even worse. But what would they do without me! Huh? Ask yourself that!"

Will crossed his arms and huffed, drawing Sienna's attention.

"And then there's you," she continued, her voice getting louder with each passing moment. "I was trying to help you most of all. I wanted you to be happy. And also, maybe then my mom would realize that I'm not an evil daughter."

"Earth to Sienna," said Will. "I don't need your help, and neither does anyone else. Maybe you should do *yourself* a favor and stop trying so hard."

"Why? So I can be like you? All . . . 'I don't care

about anything because I'm too cool to even stand up for myself.'"

"I stand up for myself," said Will.

"No," said Sienna. "You do the exact opposite. You hate the *Dr. Dad* podcast, but you're scared to tell your dad to stop. Or to confront Gavin about his horrible videos. And also, would you even be here with Lily if it wasn't for me? Huh?"

As Sienna's anger settled over their tiny table in the middle of the coffee shop, Lily's mind swirled with everything that she'd just learned. Sasha was secretly helping Sienna cheat for money. Will hated his dad's podcast. Sienna had thought they might become friends. Sienna herself felt misunderstood and left out. While this last realization softened Lily's view of Sienna, it didn't mean she was prepared to forget everything that Sienna had done. The photograph of the envelope was still on the table. Lily pushed it toward Sienna. "You have to tell everyone that I didn't steal your necklace."

Sienna rolled her eyes. "It's not a big deal, Lily."

"Yes, it is. You accused me of something I didn't do."

"Trust me. Everyone will forget about it. The dance is in two days. Date drama is way more important than a silly necklace."

Will tried to speak, but Lily continued. "It's important to me, Sienna. I want you to wear the necklace to school tomorrow so everyone can see that I didn't steal it."

"Um, he-llo." Sienna lifted the photo. "As we can clearly see, the necklace is in the trash. So number one, that's disgusting. Number two, it's probably impossible to find. And number three, I don't know what I'm wearing tomorrow and it might not work with my outfit."

"Correction," said Will. "The necklace is in the recycling. And I happen to know recycling only gets collected on Friday."

Sienna bugged out her eyes. "How do you even know that!"

Will smiled. "You get in trouble enough times, you learn things."

Lily was still mad and Sienna was still deep in her own pity party, but laughter spread around their table, drawing the attention of other customers who had no idea what they were laughing about but smiled nonetheless. Sienna was the first to catch her breath long enough to speak.

"Fine," she said. "Tomorrow morning before homeroom. I'll meet you guys there."

"Make sure you plan your outfit to match," said Will before he broke back into uncontrollable laughter.

Sienna flipped her hair over her shoulders. "Obviously."

That did it. Lily was done. She laughed harder than she had in a very long time.

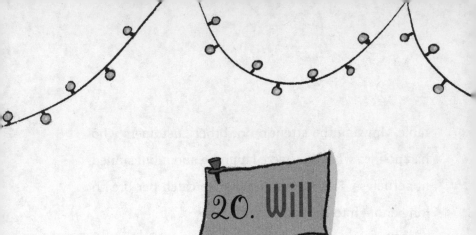

20. Will

Will's phone buzzed in his back pocket, vibrating against the metal chair.

Once, twice, three times.

He was having so much fun with Lily and (shockingly!) Sienna, that he wanted to ignore it. But it buzzed again and Will gave in, pulling the phone from his jeans. The screen lit up with a stream of texts from Gavin.

> Dude
>
> Dude!
>
> Where r u?
>
> My mom has appointment
> with her back guru
> and she can't be late

She's getting pissed

Very pissed

And I'm gonna wet my pants from fear

Crap! He was late for climbing.

Will shot back a quick text telling Gavin that he was on his way. He stood up. "I've got climbing. Gavin's waiting outside my apartment."

Sienna rolled her eyes. As if the simple mention of Gavin proved something.

Will looked at Lily. "You coming?"

She shook her head. "I think I might get a drink or something."

Will considered trying to convince her to leave. But Sienna did seem . . . different. Sort of deflated. Which was not a bad thing.

As Will sprinted down the sidewalk, he mentally kicked himself. Climbers had a reputation for being chill, which Dustin hated because he viewed climbing as a sport of precision.

Precise people were never late.

Will picked up his pace.

When he rounded the corner of his block, Gavin's car wasn't there. Will pulled his phone out of his back pocket and read the latest texts in the chain.

Not my fault

Sorry

Gavin had left without him.

It was only last week that Will had Frisbeed Gavin's phone across the courtyard. Now he was tempted to do the same with his own.

How could he be so stupid!

He'd only missed climbing practice for a stomach bug and one high fever that he couldn't hide from his dad. Speaking of . . .

"Hey there." Will's dad stepped out of their front door and leaned against the iron railing that separated their steps from their neighbor's brownstone.

"Can you give me a ride to the gym?" asked Will. "Gavin's mom left without me."

"No can do."

"What? Why?" Will scanned the block. "The car's parked right there."

"This is not about whether I *can* drive you. It's about whether I *will* drive you."

There were no headphones over his dad's ears, no microphone in front of his mouth. But the shift to *Dr. Dad* mode was full-on. He was in life lesson teaching mode.

"Come on, Dad. I was five minutes late."

His dad checked his watch. "More like fifteen."

"Give me a break."

"To what end? Have you seen the amount of money we pay every month to Philly Rocks? Because it's not a small number, Will. It's a big one. If I give you a ride, what's going to happen next time? How are you going to learn that there are consequences to your actions?"

Will threw his head back in frustration.

If Will agreed, his dad would stop talking. But he'd also take it as a victory. A lesson well taught.

He kicked his foot against the brick. When was this ever going to end?

The podcast episodes about wetting the bed. About not brushing his teeth. About all other kinds of personal things.

The intro music of his mom singing to Will before bed.

The stories. The jokes. The scripted lectures.

The secret pictures. Cool dad and little man.

He heard Sienna's comment—"You're too scared to stand up to your dad"—echo in his mind. Maybe it was time to start standing up.

Will gave his dad the middle finger.

His dad rocked backward in surprise. "Excuse me?"

Will gave him a second middle finger. His dad grabbed him by the arm and dragged Will into the common lobby, slamming the door shut behind them.

"That is unacceptable behavior, William. What is wrong with you?"

Will shot back, "What's wrong with *you*?"

His dad opened the door to their apartment. He turned to Will. "Start talking."

"Is that the way you speak to your podcast guests, Dad?"

"What does my podcast have to do with this?"

"Everything!" screamed Will. "It has everything to do with it!"

His dad sat down on the couch and clasped his hands together. Listening pose.

Will almost lost his nerve. But he'd come too far now.

"I hate everything about your podcast. I hate that you tell stories about me to millions of strangers. I hate that you take my picture without me knowing. I hate when you talk to me like you're quoting some random parenting expert. It makes me feel like you don't actually see me."

His dad stood and crouched beside him, reaching for Will's hands. "How can you say that, Will? The whole reason I created the podcast was for you. When your mom died, I was a mess. Obviously. We both were. But the thing about being a parent is there's no time to be a mess. You have to pull it together for your kid and you have to do it fast. That doesn't mean I had a clue what to do. I needed help, and the people I speak to on *Dr. Dad* are professionals who guided me through some really tough times. And yeah, lots of people listen to *Dr. Dad* because they need help, too. And in case you hadn't realized, all those people listening are what pays our bills."

"So find a different job," said Will.

"One that pays less? Or requires me to travel? Then what? Are you going to quit climbing?"

"Sure," said Will. "I'll quit climbing."

It was a lie. They both knew that.

His dad adjusted his position on the couch. "Obviously it's more complicated than that."

"Do you realize that kids in my grade listen to your show? Gavin listens to it in the car with his mom! All those stories that you think are so hilarious are actually humiliating. And also . . ." How could Will tell his dad about Lily without actually telling him anything? It was harder than hanging by a finger hold. "You really screwed things up for me with someone."

His dad bit back a smile. "This is about the girl you bought the necklace for. What's her name?"

Will shook his head. *No way* was he saying Lily's name.

"Come on, Will. I'm your dad. Let me help."

"That's the thing. You're not just my dad; you're Dr. Dad. Whatever I say becomes material for the show."

Will gave his dad time to deny it. When he didn't respond, Will stood. He walked to the front door and slammed it shut.

And then . . .

Where could he go?

Philly Rocks was miles away. Gavin wasn't home. School was closed.

Will was all alone. He missed his mom. His longing for her lodged in his lungs. Squeezing his breath. Pinching it tight.

And then the words that had been drilled into him so many times came to mind. *I'm always here if you need me.* He'd never once taken Stephanie up on the offer. But now he had no choice.

Will needed to talk. And Stephanie was the only person he could imagine opening up to.

21. Lily

While their parents were out at an "introduction to college admissions" talk, Lily and Reese ordered pizza for dinner. When Lily finished her last slice, she could no longer put off calling Sasha. As soon as her parents returned home, there was a good chance that loud arguments would echo down the apartment halls.

Of all the things that Lily had learned that afternoon, the idea of Sasha cheating was the most surprising. How had it started? And when? Lily couldn't recall ever seeing Sienna and Sasha alone together. Sienna didn't play soccer, and Sasha didn't hang out at the Secret Coffee Shop. They had nothing important in common. Lily sat on the couch and wrapped a blanket over her legs. Then she FaceTimed Sasha.

"OMG, phew," answered Sasha after just one ring.

"Perfect timing. My mom is killing me. She has a baby shower this weekend, and the parents want a duck theme. If I have to make one more tiny beak out of fondant, I'm going to . . . ." Sasha collapsed on the kitchen counter, taking the phone with her. Lily heard Sasha beg her mom for a break.

Moments later Sasha was in her bedroom, the phone close to her face. "What's up, Lil? Should I add Maddie? We had a light soccer practice today. For, like, the first time in *forever*."

"That's okay," said Lily. "I just wanted to talk to you."

Sasha's eyes stopped wandering around her room and focused on the screen. "Oh, why?"

"It's about math."

"Gotcha. Need help with your homework? We could do it together over the phone."

Lily almost lost her nerve. Maybe this was all a misunderstanding, and Sasha had simply offered to help Sienna in a friendly, casual way. Not a cheating way. Only that didn't explain the secretive exchange of envelopes and, worst of all, Sienna's claim that she'd paid Sasha for her work. Lily missed Maddie's commanding presence. It was hard to do this alone.

"Actually," continued Lily as she wrapped the blanket tight, "it's about math and Sienna. Sienna said she pays you for answers to her math homework. But obviously that's not true, right?"

Lily was left staring at the ceiling. Then came the sound of a door closing. When Sasha returned, she spoke in a whisper. "Sienna told you that? When?"

"This afternoon."

"Were you guys alone?"

Lily shook her head. "Will was there."

"Oh my God," said Sasha. "I'm going to *kill* her. Sienna promised. She promised, like, one million times that she would never, ever tell a single person as long as she lived. I don't know why I trusted her. I don't know why. . . ." Sasha wiped her cheek with the side of her hand. Lily couldn't make out the tears over the screen, but the quiver in Sasha's voice confirmed they were there.

"But why would you do it, Sash? You could get in so much trouble."

"It's not like cheating on a test," said Sasha. "It's just homework. People get help all the time, from their parents and tutors or whatever. Do you really think Jake gets through school all by himself? Because I seriously doubt that."

Sienna had used the same justification. And while it made sense, something was off about the excuse.

"But it's Sienna," said Lily. "You don't even like her."

"So what! I don't like a lot of things! Actually, I *hate* a lot of things! I hate how everyone else always has loads of money for candy and coffee or whatever, and I always have to beg my mom for change. I hate how guilty I feel because of how hard my mom works for every single dollar. I hate barely making the elite team and everyone knowing it because I'm a benchwarmer while Maddie is the top scorer. I hate how Maddie is always texting on her phone during carpool but she never shows me who she's texting. Just because I hate Sienna doesn't mean I can't deal with her like I deal with everything else. At least she pays me."

Now Lily could see the tears. She wished she was there to give Sasha a hug. They'd been best friends for so long, but Lily couldn't remember ever seeing Sasha cry like this. Still, there was more Lily needed to know. "But why'd you mess her up with the wrong answers?" she asked.

"I just did it one time. I was worried Mr. Myron would get suspicious if Sienna started getting everything right all of a sudden. And if Sienna got in trouble, you know she'd tell on me right away."

Lily nodded. Sasha was right about that.

"Please don't tell Maddie," said Sasha.

"I won't," said Lily. "I promise."

Sasha looked away from the screen, hesitating. "Do you know who Maddie's always secretly texting? Is it Theo?"

So Maddie still hadn't told Sasha about Bex. Just like Sasha didn't want to tell Maddie about this. Would all these secrets be revealed? Maybe someday. But one thing was certain: neither was Lily's secret to tell. "I don't know," said Lily. "Have you tried asking her?"

Sasha shook her head.

The release of the front door lock drew Lily's

attention. "My parents are home," she said. "I should probably go."

"Okay," said Sasha. "I'm going to call Maddie. Since you already know, I might tell her about Sienna. I'm not sure. Is it okay with you if I call her alone?"

"Sure," said Lily. "Text me to tell me how it goes."

Lily's parents greeted her with a kiss. She expected them to continue into the kitchen, where Reese was at the counter, and launch into whatever lecture they'd been devising on the walk home. Instead, her mom plopped down beside her on the couch. Lily leaned against her, soaking in the familiarity of her body.

"Reese," called their mom as she wrapped one arm around Lily's shoulders and squeezed. "Can you come in here? I'm calling a family meeting."

"Do I have to?" asked Reese.

Their mom and dad answered in unison: "Yes!"

"Geez," said Reese. "I'm coming. Chill out."

"Actually," said their mom, "that's kind of what we were thinking about doing."

"Um . . . what happened at school?" asked Reese

as she sat on a chair facing the couch. "Did you guys get swapped with other parents. Is this one of those movies where you're trapped in the wrong bodies?"

Their dad laughed. "Unfortunately not. We're still us."

"But we're going to try something new," added their mom. She went on to explain about their evening and all the parents who were complaining about their children's lack of ambition and drive. "And it occurred to me that maybe we've been too hard on you." Their dad cleared his throat. "Okay, fine," continued their mom. "Maybe *I've* been too hard on you."

Their dad motioned for her to keep going. Lily's mom removed her arm from Lily's shoulders and focused entirely on Reese. "One of the panelists tonight was from the Fashion Institute of Technology. She was very professional and well-spoken—"

"Wow, Mom," interrupted Reese. "Way to hide your surprise."

"Let your mother finish, Reese," said their dad.

"So after the presentation I went up to her and introduced myself."

Reese buried her face in her hands. "Oh my God, tell me that you didn't."

Their mom nodded. "I did indeed. I told her that my daughter has a social media account dedicated to her love of fashion."

"Stop," said Reese. "Please stop."

"I even pulled it up on my phone and . . ." Reese spread her fingers, peeking out nervously. "She loved it, honey. She was so impressed. She gave me her card and said she wants you to reach out directly."

Reese jumped to her feet. "What! No way."

"It's true," said their dad. "I was standing right there. Your mom was great."

Their mom shook her head. "It had nothing to do with me. It was all you, Reese. All your dedication and determination. I don't know much about fashion, but I know work ethic. You have the kind of drive and passion that can't be taught. I'm sorry that it's taken me this long to see it."

Reese walked over to the couch and their mom stood up. Their hug was long and hard. Lily had no idea how long this peace would last. Maybe one day. Maybe one week. Maybe one year. Lily jumped up and wrapped her arms around them both, grateful that at least it was happening now.

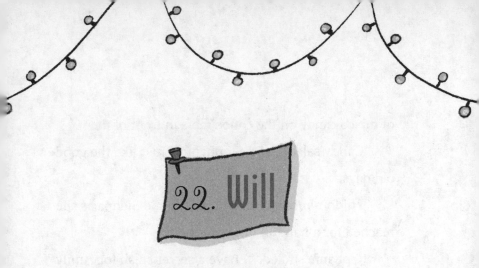

22. Will

Stephanie answered Will's call on the first ring. Sienna was home, so they met on a bench outside the apartment building. Will told Stephanie almost everything. He left out what Sienna had said at the Secret Coffee Shop.

That was Sienna's story to tell. If she wanted to.

When Will was all talked out, he agreed to follow Stephanie up to the apartment for dinner. His eyes were still red from tears, but Sienna didn't make a big deal out of it. They spent most of dinner scrolling on their phones. Stephanie was too busy talking on the phone with Will's dad behind the closed doors of her bedroom to care.

Now it was getting dark. Will sat on one end of the couch. Sienna sat on the other. Stephanie placed a bowl of mixed candy on the coffee table in front of them.

"Candy salad," said Stephanie. "Just like the good old days."

"I didn't know we had all this," said Sienna as she reached for a handful of gummies.

Stephanie smiled. "I have a secret stash for family emergencies." She leaned over to kiss Will on the head. "And yes, Will. Like it or not, you're family."

"You can choose 'not,'" said Sienna. "I'd understand."

They all cracked up. Will threw a gummy bear at Sienna's head. She threw a jelly bean back.

As the laughter faded, Stephanie checked her phone. She sighed. "It's time, Will. You're welcome to spend the night, but you've got to call your dad first."

"Okay," said Will. "But I'm just going to text him instead."

Stephanie began to protest, saying that a phone call would be much better. Sienna stopped her. "Mom," she said, placing her hand on Stephanie's arm. "Let Will do it however he wants. He's got this."

"Okay," said Stephanie, squeezing Sienna's hand

with a sigh. "You're right. You two are older now. I forget that."

Will walked to the farthest end of the hall and slid against the wall, sinking down to the floor. With his phone between his knees, he texted:

Hey Dad

The reply was instant.

Will! I'm so sorry. Please
come home. I really
want to talk.

Not in the mood to talk
I'm going to sleep at
Stephanie's tonight

Please Will. I want
to figure this out.

So do I, thought Will. More than anything.

But Will had already done a lot of talking today. Mr. Stanlow. His dad. Stephanie.

Trying to get adults to see his side of things was exhausting.

When Will didn't respond, his dad texted:

> I'm going to tone it down.
> I promise. I understand
> where you're coming from.
> I won't say or post anything
> without your approval.
> How does that sound?

Like more of the same, thought Will. Except even more complicated. If Will said no to something, would his dad be upset? Would he blame Will if his podcast ratings went down? If his Instagram followers left?

> It sounds like you don't get it

> I do. Honestly. I think you're
> just tired Will. It's been
> a long day. Let's both get
> some sleep and talk
> about it tomorrow.

Suddenly Will wasn't tired. He was angry. And determined. It was time to be perfectly clear.

> I need you to listen to me
> Dad
> Toning it down is not good
> enough
> My life is my life
> You can't share it anymore
> At all
> That's all you need to know
> There's nothing else to talk
> about

The dots of his dad's typing appeared. Disappeared. Then appeared once more.

> OK Will. I love you.

Will locked his phone and exhaled, dropping his head between his knees.

When he looked up, Sienna and Stephanie were there. Sienna sat on one side of him, Stephanie on the other.

"Sorry," said Will, wiping his eyes.

"You've got nothing to apologize for," said Stephanie. "I was just telling Sienna that your mom would be really proud of you, Will. And I'm proud, too. Of both of you."

Sienna gave her mom a sideways glance. *Both?*

Stephanie nodded. "I know I'm hard on you, honey, but it's only because I worry so much. Sometimes all that worrying makes me blind to the good things, like the two of you being there for each other through all the ups and downs." Stephanie grinned. "Even if being there involves throwing candy."

"Will threw it first," said Sienna.

"Did not," said Will.

Stephanie clapped her hands on her thighs. "And now it's officially time for bed." She stood and offered them each a hand, pulling them in for a big hug. Behind Stephanie's back, Sienna stuck out her tongue at Will. He returned the gesture.

There was a ton that he was desperate to change. But some things would always stay the same.

23. Lily and Will (and Sienna)

They met outside the trash room on Thursday morning. Lily got there first, followed by Will and Sienna. Lily assumed it was a coincidence that Will and Sienna arrived at the exact same time. But as they got closer, she wondered if they'd carpooled. Why else would they be so quiet?

"Hey, Lily," said Will.

"Hey," she replied. There was embarrassment beneath Will's tilted half smile. Something had pushed yesterday's silliness out of the way.

"I'm just gonna step over here," said Sienna, tiptoeing a few feet down the hall. "You two, you know, talk or whatever."

"What's going on?" asked Lily. She'd last seen Will sprinting down the street to go climbing.

Maybe he'd gotten hurt at practice?

"I slept at Sienna's last night," said Will. "I had a big fight with my dad and I didn't want to go home. Sienna's mom helped me figure some stuff out. I'll probably go back home tonight. I'm not sure yet."

Lily nodded. "Wow. Thanks for telling me."

"I told him you would understand," whisper-shouted Sienna from down the hall where she was pretending not to listen.

"I do," said Lily. "I mean, not all of it. But I want to."

"Thanks," said Will. "That's really cool." Then he called to Sienna, "I thought you were going to stay out of it."

"Ugh, Will. When are you going to understand that you need my help."

Will threw his head back in frustration. "Never."

Sienna smirked. "Puh-lease. Keep dreaming."

Whatever had happened last night placed them right back in sibling mode. But where did that leave Lily? Exactly, she realized, as she was. Their relationship didn't affect her. She didn't have to take sides. She could be friendly with Sienna *and* stack up a whole load of private jokes with Will. Maybe they would even all go to the dance together tomorrow.

Before any of that, however, Lily needed to put an end to the necklace rumors.

"So," she said, looking from Sienna to the trash room door. "Are you ready?"

"About that," said Sienna. "I've been thinking. I'm not sure digging through trash is, like, the vibe I'm going for today. How about we do this tomorrow? Or maybe next week?"

"Or maybe never?" added Will jokingly.

"Exactly!"

"No way," said Lily. "We're finding that necklace and you're wearing it. *Today.*"

"Fine," said Sienna, pinching her nose. "But if I barf, it's game over. And just so you know, I have a very sensitive gag reflex."

Will rolled his eyes as he pushed open the door. Sienna surveyed the room full of large bins, appearing pleasantly surprised. The room was cleaner than Lily had expected. As Will pointed to the bin where he suggested Sienna should start digging, Lily checked the time. Homeroom started in seven minutes. That morning Maddie and Sasha had texted on the group chat that they wanted to meet up by their lockers. Lily had promised to try.

Now, she looked to Will. "There's somewhere I need to be. Can you . . . ?"

"Don't worry," said Will. "I've got this."

Sienna stood in the middle of the large recycling bin, her hands on her hips. "What do you mean, *I've* got this? You're not even helping! You're just, like, standing."

"Well, duh," said Will. "You're the helpful one, remember, Sienna?"

Lily laughed as she left the trash room. She passed Mr. Stanlow, who was rearranging a bulletin board, and then turned down the hallway to the seventh grade lockers, almost running right into Gavin.

"Hey, Lily," he said. "Have you seen Will? He's gone MIA. Like, way off the grid." When Lily shook her head Gavin continued, "I think he's ghosting me. Why would he do that?"

"Why don't you just ask him," said Lily.

Gavin wiggled his fingers. "Like some kind of deep, dark confessional thing?"

"No," said Lily, "like a friend."

She left a confused Gavin and kept walking. Maddie and Sasha were standing at her locker. Had they talked last night? Had Maddie told Sasha about Rex, and had Sasha told Maddie about Sienna? Lily couldn't tell from their body language and, regardless, it wasn't the reason that she'd rushed to find them.

"Lily!" said Maddie.

"Yay!" squealed Sasha, turning around in delight.

It was nothing out of the ordinary. Which was the best part about it.

Lily smiled and said, "Thanks, guys."

"For what?" asked Maddie.

"Just being worried about me. And being my friends."

"Of course!" said Maddie and Sasha in unison.

They all laughed as Maddie called jinx on Sasha and Sasha protested by popping her hip into Maddie's. So they *had* talked last night. Lily smiled with relief.

Then her phone buzzed with a text from Will. It was a picture of Sienna standing next to the recycling bin, a white envelope raised over her head like a trophy, her tongue stuck out in annoyance. The caption said:

SCORE!

Lily smiled and slid the phone back into her pocket without showing it to Maddie and Sasha. When they got back from the Jubilee tournament, she'd tell them the entire story of the necklace, the sleepover, and her now-official crush on Will. Maybe by then Lily would know how it all ended. Or maybe a whole new story was just beginning.